D1255475

The Snarkout Boys & The Avocado of Death

The Snarkout Boys & The Avocado of Death

Daniel Pinkwater

Lothrop, Lee & Shepard Books • New York

Library of Congress Cataloging in Publication Data
Pinkwater, Daniel Manus, (date)
The Snarkout Boys & the avocado of death.
Summary: Walter and Winston set out to rescue the inventor
of the Alligatron, a computer developed from an avocado
which is the world's last defense against the space-realtors. [1.
Science fiction] I. Title. II. Title: Snarkout Boys and the avo-
cado of death.
PZ7.P6335Sn   [Fic]   81-11737
ISBN 0-688-00871-2   AACR2

TO BARBARA LALICKI

I

I thought that going to high school was going to be a big improvement over what I was used to. It turned out to be just the opposite. For example, there's the biology notebook. The biology notebook is what we do in my biology class. Every page in every kid's notebook is exactly the same as every page in every other kid's notebook. We have to copy out these long, boring things the teacher writes on the blackboard. And we have to copy pictures from the textbook. One of the assignments is to copy the picture of a grasshopper and letter in all the labels showing what the different parts of the grasshopper are. The labels are in the textbook, too. When the notebook is all finished, we're supposed to put it in a folder and make a nice cover. We can put anything we like on the cover. If the cover is really nice and artistic, you'll get an A on the notebook— and for the course. If you copy everything you're supposed to and the cover is only so-so, you'll get a B. A kid with sloppy handwriting, one who can't draw, might get a C.

I would say that the biology notebook is typical of what goes on at Genghis Khan High School.

I've been going to that school for eight months, and I

still can't believe how utterly boring, nauseating, stupid, and generally crummy it is. I don't have a single class I like. I don't have a single teacher who's the least bit interesting. What's worse, most of the kids don't seem to care that the school stinks. They don't like it, but they aren't outraged about it. They just go through the motions—like robots, or zombies. The big thing for most of the kids is getting into various kinds of trouble outside of school. For my part, getting hold of beer and throwing up every weekend isn't any more interesting than the school.

I think I might have gone crazy in that miserable school if I hadn't gotten to be friends with Winston Bongo.

Winston Bongo is a very creative person. He's the inventor of Snarking Out. He also holds the world's record for number of Snark Outs successfully completed. Until he invented Snarking, no one on Earth had ever Snarked, as far as we knew. And until I became a Snarker, Winston was the only person to do it.

I have the second greatest number of Snarks to my credit, but I have no solo Snarks at all. So, I guess you could say that I was the co-inventor of team Snarking.

I met Winston Bongo on the first day of Mrs. Macmillan's English class. He came in late. He'd gotten delayed trying to borrow a Jewish star to wear to class. This is one of the few positive things that I've noticed at Genghis Khan High School. This Mrs. Macmillan has something against Jews. Years ago, she used to make speeches about Jews in her classroom. So this tradition got started: Every semester, kids who aren't Jewish, and Jewish kids who don't have them, borrow Jewish stars to wear around their necks in Mrs. Macmillan's class. It's fun to watch her panic when she realizes that she's facing another all-Jewish class. She believes that Jews creep around, plotting the end of civilization—and seeing all those Stars of David makes her crazy.

The first time I met Winston Bongo was in that class, on the first day. He walked in and tripped. He fell to the floor with more noise than I would have thought possible for one kid to make just falling down. It sounded like a chest of drawers falling down stairs.

I didn't know who he was at the time, but I noticed that he was sort of heavy and thick in his body. His black hair looked like it had been cropped with dog clippers. His nose was long and fat at the same time, and his eyes seemed to wander against his will.

"The poor kid is retarded," I thought. "I'll be nice to him."

Winston Bongo gathered up the books and pencils and sheets of paper he'd strewn everywhere when he fell. He sat down in the seat next to mine.

Later on, I would find out what Winston Bongo thought when he first saw me. "The poor kid is retarded," Winston thought. "I'll be nice to him." The fact is, I probably look as weird as Winston Bongo. I'm about the shortest kid in school. Also the fattest. People refer to me as No Neck. It's my nickname. I don't care for it. I happen to look like a penguin. Is that so bad?

The other thing that makes Winston Bongo appear to be not right in the head is this funny smile he's got. When he was taking that incredibly loud and clumsy fall, he was smiling, sort of to himself, no teeth showing.

It turns out that Winston Bongo is a fantastic wrestler.

He's taken private lessons at a professional gym, and he knows hundreds of falls and tumbles. His uncle is a professional wrestler. You can see him on television sometimes. His name is the Mighty Gorilla.

Of course, I didn't know any of this that day. I didn't know that Winston Bongo had taken the fall to amuse himself—on purpose. I just thought he was a big klutz.

After class, Winston Bongo looked at me. From the way he was looking, I thought he was going to make some remark—like calling me No Neck, or Fire Plug. I had this momentary feeling of anger and humiliation. Here I was about to be insulted by a kid who was obviously feeble-minded and had fallen over his own feet not a half hour before. But he didn't say anything insulting. "You ever do any wrestling? he asked. "You've got the build for it."

II

Winston Bongo lives in an apartment building about a block from the one I live in. His building is slightly more complicated to Snark Out of, because they have an elevator man. In my building the elevator is self-service. That makes Snarking Out less of a challenge.

Winston Bongo has to sneak down eleven flights of the service stairs and then slip past the little room where the elevator man sits watching the late movie on television. All I have to do is get dressed in the dark, get out of the apartment without waking my parents, take the self-service elevator to the basement garage, and go out a side exit so the night watchman in the lobby won't see me.

Then I meet Winston Bongo, and we take the Snark Street bus all the way downtown and get off across the street from the Snark Theater.

That's the main part—the technical part—of Snarking Out, except for the hats, of course. You have to wear a hat when Snarking Out. The idea is to keep anyone from guessing that you're underage when you ride the bus or buy your tickets at the Snark Theater. I question whether this works, or whether anybody cares that we're kids. We've each got a fake student activity card from Hun State University. Winston got them from his sister, who goes there. Mine has a girl's picture on it and is fixed up with ballpoint pen. It wouldn't fool anybody if they looked at it closely, but nobody ever does. And we get the student discount—fifty cents at all times—at the Snark.

Still, Winston invented Snarking Out, and he insists on hats. They have to have brims, so we can keep our faces in shadow. I have a cowboy hat, and Winston has a regular snap-brim his father used to wear years ago.

The Snark Theater has a different double bill every day, and it's open twenty-four hours around the clock. It shows movies I never heard of, and it shows them in strange combinations.

For example, a typical double bill might consist of a Yugoslavian film (with subtitles), *Vampires in a Deserted Seaside Hotel at the End of August,* and along with it, *In-*

vasion of the Bageloids, in which rock-hard, intelligent bagels from outer space attack Earth. Everybody gets bopped on the head until the scientists figure out a way to defeat the bageloids. I won't spoil the ending by telling what it is, but it has something to do with cream cheese.

I wouldn't say that every movie the Snark Theater shows is good, but they're all interesting in their way.

Another nifty thing about the Snark Theater is that there's a box in the lobby: You can write down the name of any film that was ever made and drop the slip of paper in the box, and the Snark Theater will get that film and show it. They send you a letter with a free ticket on the day they show the film you asked for. And if you tell them your birthday, they send you a free ticket on your birthday.

Winston Bongo found out about a movie from his uncle, the Mighty Gorilla. It was a film his uncle had seen once when he was wrestling in Germany. It was called *The Beethoven Story*—the life story of Ludwig van Beethoven. Winston requested it, and a couple of months later we Snarked Out and saw it. Winston saw it for free. We are always looking for obscure, unknown films to ask for. The difficult part is finding out about those films, unknown as they are.

Of course, we could go to the Snark Theater at ordinary times instead of slipping out of the house when our parents are sleeping—but that wouldn't be Snarking Out.

On a typical Snarking Out evening, I go home right after school and do my idiotic homework. While doing that, I like to listen to the radio. Lately, I've become something of a classical-music freak. There's this radio station,

WGNU, that plays all kinds of classical music. My favorite composer is this guy named Mozart.

My parents don't go in for much music at all. Once in a while they watch a singer on television, and that's about it. In addition to doing my mindless homework and listening to some music, I feed my bird and clean up his cage. My bird is a parakeet. I bought him in the dime store. I also got him a king-sized cage, so he won't feel too crowded. When I'm home, I close the door to my room and let him fly around. His name is Nosferatu. He used to be called Pete. Pete Parakeet. I changed his name after I saw this old movie at the Snark. It's called *Nosferatu*, and it's the original Dracula story. It's ten times as scary as the version you see on television. The guy who plays the vampire is really bizarre. My parakeet is sort of bizarre, too. He's pale and skinny, if you can imagine a skinny parakeet. He looks like he's in bad health, but he's really all right. I've had him for about three years, and the whole time he's looked as if he might drop dead any minute, so I renamed him Nosferatu, after the skinny vampire in the movie.

My parents weren't too happy about my bringing home a pet. Also, my mother said that birds are bad luck.

You have to watch out for her. She makes up superstitions on the spur of the moment. For example, I actually believed it was bad luck to get a haircut on Thursdays until I was about eleven years old. I might have believed it longer, but I noticed that my mother had changed the unlucky day to Tuesday. She also told me that if you eat cherries and drink milk at the same time, you'll be dead within half an hour. I think one time someone she knew, maybe her boss where she worked, ate some cherry pie and a glass of milk and then happened to die a little while later. It's hard to track these things down, because if you question my mother directly, about anything, she gets cagey and denies everything. She says she's not superstitious.

III

On the evening I'm telling about now, my father called me to supper. "Walter! Come see what I've got."

What he had was an avocado. Whenever he brings one home, which is fairly often, he makes a big fuss about it.

"Looky, Walter, an avocado! What do you think of it?" My father is the only person I know who says "looky!" He also says "lookit!"

What I think of avocados is this: On principle, I do not eat green, slimy things. My mother doesn't eat them either. She says she doesn't like the taste of avocado. That's good enough for me. If there's any question at all about the taste, I'm leaving those suckers alone.

My father loves them. Every time he brings one home, he acts like it's a three-hundred-pound sailfish he's caught singlehanded, or an elk he brought down with a bow and arrow.

He's really enthusiastic about avocados. He skins them and digs out that oversized, stupid-looking pit, and then mashes up the slimy green part with a fork. Then he puts lemon juice and vinegar, salt and pepper, and powdered garlic and paprika on it. If you have to go to all that trouble to disguise the flavor, why bother, I say.

Then he makes a speech about it. "My goodness, this is one fine avocado," he says. "You have to know how to choose them. You have to look for the ones that are black and blasted looking. The pretty green ones aren't fit to eat. The funny thing is that they reduce the price of the really scrumptious ones just because they're ugly. I guess they want to sell them before they rot completely."

My father isn't a bad guy, in my opinion. There are just a few subjects, like avocados, on which he's irrational.

My mother had found another tuna-casserole recipe. This is something of a hobby with her. She's constantly finding these recipes in women's magazines. She tries another one at least once a week. They all taste like tuna fish. Usually they have things in them you wouldn't expect to eat with tuna fish—like grapes, hot-pickle slices, fried Chinese noodles.

"I hope you will appreciate this, kiddo," my mother says, "seeing that your mother took a healthy slice out of her finger whilst chopping up the ingredients." She usually manages to injure herself at least once while preparing a meal. She has a Band-Aid on her finger.

"Eat up, champ," she says. "It's American." My mother has an idea that tuna caught in Japanese waters is tainted with radioactivity, so she always shops for brands canned within the continental United States. Even Canadian brands are out. "They're too chummy with the Common-ists," she says. She calls Communists "Commonists."

If you were blind, or only knew my mother from talk-ing with her on the telephone, you'd probably think she was about six feet tall . . . and maybe two hundred and fifty pounds in weight. It's her voice, and the way she talks. She sounds like she ought to be a big, slow-moving person, maybe a little sloppy. Actually, she's small and nervous, al-ways well dressed, and a chain smoker. Once my father and I have started eating our meal, she brings a little ash-tray to the table and puffs a cigarette between bites of food. This is far more disgusting than avocado eating. If I can possibly get out of it, I try not to have meals with my parents. I've complained to them about various nauseating things they do, but it doesn't do any good. "Everybody has a family," my mother says. I don't know what that means.

Our apartment is new. We are the first people ever to live in it. When we first moved into the building, it wasn't quite finished. The whole place smelled of paint, and there was brown paper on the floors in the elevator and the hallways. In those days, we had to take our shoes off out-side the apartment door so we wouldn't track plaster dust onto the carpet.

Come to think of it, I've never walked on the carpet in our living room. There are these clear plastic runners my mother put down, making a kind of path through the liv-ing room to the dining alcove. The furniture has plastic covers, too. My mother says that when you decorate with light colors, you have to be careful. Nobody ever sits in the living room, except when my parents have company

—and then it has to be company wearing suits and ties, and fancy dresses. When they expect company like that, my father puts on a suit and tie, and my mother puts on a fancy dress and rolls up the plastic runners, and they all sit in the living room. I get called in to be introduced to the company. I always stand at the edge of the living-room carpet. The company says, "I understand you're a fine young man," or, "He looks like a football player. Are you a football player?" I'm at least a foot too short to be a football player. Besides which, I hate football.

"Yes," I say, "I'm a football player." This happens—having company in the living room—about twice a year. The rest of the time, nobody sits there.

When regular people—relatives and such—come over, everybody sits in the den. The den has a linoleum floor. Sometimes my father sits around in his undershirt. When he's feeling funny, he gets Nosferatu and gets him to sit on his head. Apparently, Nosferatu likes him. He'll sit on my father's head for an hour.

IV

The secret of Snarking Out on a school night is to get to bed extra early and then wake up in time to Snark—usually about 1:00 A.M. The problem is this: If you don't wake up in the time to Snark, your Snarking partner will be standing in the street at one in the morning, waiting for you. That would be poor form. However, if you set the alarm clock, it might wake up your parents.

This is how I solved the problem. I wrap my electric alarm clock in three or four undershirts and close it in a dresser drawer. When it goes off, the sound is muffled. You can't hear it outside my bedroom. I tried this out one day when my parents were out of the house.

Usually, I wake up just before the alarm clock is set to go off. I don't know why that is, but anytime I want to get up at a specific hour, I usually wake up at that hour. Those times I don't wake up, the tiny, muffled sound coming from my dresser wakes me. I stop the thing from sounding by pulling out the plug—otherwise, it would get louder as I open the drawer and unwrap it to get at the little button on the back. Also, I don't want it to go on buzzing too long, just in case one of my parents is sleeping lightly.

I take the unplugged alarm clock out of the dresser drawer and push the little button that stops it from sounding. Then, by the light coming from the streetlamps outside (we are only on the sixth floor—my mother won't live any higher because, she says, the fall from any higher is sure to be fatal) I reset the clock for the time I usually get up for school. I get dressed and put a pillow and a bunch of clothes and things in the bed to look like me in case anyone wakes up and peeks in. Then I sneak out.

On this particular occasion, I went to bed a little before nine o'clock. That's fairly early, I know, but it doesn't make my parents suspicious because they seldom stay up past eleven themselves. Also, I make a point of going to bed at all different times, to keep them off guard. When I get up at one in the morning, I already have had half a night's sleep. Then, if I can get back from Snarking between four and five, I can catch another three hours and wind up with a total of seven. I read in my hygiene book last year that you really need no less than eight, but I can get by with seven once in a while. Besides, at Genghis Khan High School, being half asleep helps kill the pain of spending a whole day with nothing worthwhile to do.

Actually, on this particular night I woke up at five minutes to one. I don't want to seem to be boasting, but my Snarking technique is so developed that I can be up, dressed, and out of the house in five minutes without making a sound.

It went without a hitch. I was in the street four minutes and forty-six seconds later, which equaled my best time previously. I have a stop watch right next to the bed, and the first thing I do when Snarking Out is punch the stop watch, and later slip it, still running, into my pocket.

Winston Bongo arrived a few seconds later, stop watch in hand. He pushed the button as he came up to the bus stop. "How long did it take you?" I asked.

"Seven minutes even." It takes him longer than me because he has to use the stairs and get past the elevator man. Still, seven minutes is very respectable, world-class Snarking time.

"The bus will be along at one-o-three," he said.

We had our hats on.

The bus was on time. We got on, paid our fares, and went to sit in the back. There was nobody else on board.

As the Snark Street bus got farther downtown, a few people got on and off. A lot of them were people we'd come to recognize from other rides on the Snark Street bus. There was an old black man with a chicken, for example. We've seen him lots of times.

"Do you know what's playing tonight?" I asked Winston Bongo. Usually I check the newspaper, but tonight I forgot.

"It's a Laurel and Hardy festival," he said.

"That's good." I like Laurel and Hardy. They have their movies on television sometimes, but they're always cut so they will fit in the half-hour kiddie-show format—and half of that is commercials for toys and breakfast cereals.

When we got to the Snark Theater, the place was packed. It was hard to find two seats together. Where did all these people come from at after one in the morning? Usually the Snark is a little less than half full at this hour.

And the audience was going crazy. They were laughing and hollering and carrying on. I'd never seen anything like it.

When we came in they were showing a movie—just ending—in which Laurel and Hardy are destroying this guy's house, and the guy is destroying their car. It's pretty funny, but not nearly funny enough to account for all the screaming and laughing. That was because we came in at the end. By the time the next movie came to the end we were screaming and hollering, too.

I've never had so much fun at the movies. As each new film started, and the audience heard the Laurel and Hardy theme song, everybody started cheering and clapping. We did it, too.

The thing about Laurel and Hardy movies that you can't get from the chopped-up versions on television is how beautiful they are. Things happen exactly at the moment they have to happen. They don't happen a second too soon or too late. You can even predict what's going to happen—and it does happen—and it surprises you anyway. It doesn't surprise you because it happened, but because it happened so perfectly. I laughed so hard that I cried.

Winston Bongo and I did something that night that we had never done before. There was even some question as to whether it was against the International Snarking Rules. What we did was leave the Snark Theater before the performance was over. Of course, there was a technicality involved—we didn't actually leave during the course of a film, but we left before all the films on the program had been shown.

The reason we did that was that we simply had enough. We didn't have the strength to laugh anymore. It was like eating five pieces of the best cake in the world—you just can't handle number six.

When we came out of the Snark Theater, we were staggering around, weak from all that laughing. Also, we felt sort of disappointed that we didn't have the strength to stay for the rest of the films. In the lobby, we noticed a sign we hadn't seen coming in. It said that anyone who had the time they went in stamped on their ticket stub could have his money back if he stayed through the whole program. So we weren't the only ones. That made us feel a little better.

Winston couldn't contain himself and did several very good falls while we were waiting for the bus.

Also, I love Laurel and Hardy because Hardy's fat, and I'm fat, and Winston Bongo isn't exactly a beanpole either.

V

It was only about two-thirty in the morning, a lot earlier than we usually got out of the Snark Theater. There was another hour and a half, at least, of Laurel and Hardy films that we weren't going to see. On the bus going home, we discussed whether to count this as a completed Snark Out or not. There was some talk about counting it as a half Snark, but that would always look sloppy on our records. Finally we decided, since we left the theater voluntarily, and had completed the sneaking out, and would, hopefully, complete the sneaking in, that this could count as a full Snark.

Then the bus broke down. There was a grinding noise, and it rolled to a stop. The driver fiddled around at the controls for a while and then spoke to the passengers. That was us, and the old black guy, the one with the chicken who had been on the bus with us coming the other way. This was a live chicken, by the way. The old guy is a familiar sight in the streets of Baconburg. Sometimes he makes the chicken perform for people.

"Look, folks," the bus driver said, "we seem to be stuck. If you like, I can give you a refund, or you can wait until the next bus comes in about twenty minutes, and I'll give you a transfer slip so you can ride it for free."

It was a nice night. "We're about halfway home," Winston Bongo said to me. "What do you say we walk the rest of the way? It's still early."

It was an unusually mild night for April. I agreed—we'd get a refund and walk home. The old guy with the chicken had decided to get off the bus, too. The bus driver gave us back our money, and we stepped off onto the sidewalk.

We were at the place where Snark Street takes a bend to the left. Across the street was Blueberry Park and the Blueberry Library. I'd ridden past this place lots of times, but I'd never been here on foot. It's an old part of town with lots of trees and old-fashioned little buildings, three or four stories tall, with steps going up from the sidewalk to the front doors.

Late as it was, there were quite a few people in the park. Some were sitting on benches, talking. There was a chess game going on under the streetlights, and a little crowd of people was standing around, listening to someone give a speech.

Blueberry Park and the library next to it were left to the city of Baconburg by James Blueberry, the toothpick millionaire. For a long time, the Blueberry Toothpick Works was the biggest industry in Baconburg. When Mr. Blueberry left the park to the city, he made certain conditions about the use of the place. In his will, it said that the city could have the park, as long as people were permitted to speak there. Anyone who wants to can make a speech there. He or she can say anything at all, and no one is allowed to stop the speech. They don't have to have a permit or anything like that. The other condition Mr. Blueberry made was that there was to be a wall around the park. The city got around that by building a little wall—only a foot high—all around the park. But anybody can make a speech there.

The tall old man in the raincoat—the one with the chicken—wandered across the street and joined the crowd listening to the speaker. Winston Bongo and I went over, too.

The guy giving the speech was a short guy in a raincoat. He had a thick black beard, and glasses.

"Cats and kitties," the guy was saying, "be hip to my lick. My wig may be uncool, but my jive is solid."

"What's he talking about?" I asked Winston Bongo.

"I don't know," Winston Bongo said.

"The Man is putting us little cats down," the guy in the raincoat was saying, "but us little cats are frantic, crazy, and gone. If we don't make the gig, then the gig is no-where!"

"Solid!" "Groovy!" people in the crowd called out.

"What does that mean?" Winston Bongo asked.

"I don't know," I said. "I didn't get a word of it."

"So if The Man says, 'Blow!' and us little cats don't dig the riff, all we have to say is 'Nowhere!' 'Later!' And that, cats and kitties, would be HEA-VY! So if we don't dig the flip, or the number, or the place his wig is at, we just take five until The Man cools it."

"Is he speaking English?" I asked Winston Bongo.

"The speaker is a hipster," someone said. It was the old black guy with the chicken. "He is also a trade unionist. He is discussing the possibility of a strike at the Wana-mopo Banjo Pick Factory. Many of these people are his fellow workers. What he has been saying, roughly, is this: Listen to what I have to say. My intellect may be limited,

24

but my feelings are sincere. The employers are imposing on the workers, but the workers are very important. If we don't cooperate, then the factory can't produce anything. If the employers tell us to work, and we refuse, that will constitute a great disadvantage for the employers. So, if we don't approve of the tactics, or the ideas, or the attitude of management, we can go on strike until an agreeable offer is forthcoming."

"That's what he said?" Winston Bongo exclaimed.

"More or less," said the tall, old black guy with the chicken. "He's regarded as a very good speaker. I'm afraid I don't do his words justice."

"Well, thanks," we said, and moved through the crowd to the edge of the park. As we crossed the street we could hear the crowd clapping, and shouting, "Groovy! Groo-vee!"

About half a block up the street, we could see a puddle of very bright, very yellow light. As we got closer, we saw that it was a hot-dog stand with a sort of glass enclosure in front of it. There was a flickering blue neon sign in the window that said ED AND FRED'S RED HOTS.

We went inside the glass enclosure. There was a counter made of stainless steel and two windows through which you could be served a hot dog. "Two with everything," we said.

The guy behind the counter put together two hot dogs for us. They were somewhat fatter than the usual hot dog, and very red in color. Also, they had the greenest pickle relish on them I had ever seen, as well as mustard, chopped onions, and little bits of tomato. All the lights in the place were these yellow fluorescent lights—the kind that are supposed to keep bugs away—and there were a lot of them. This made the brightly colored hot dogs and relish look even stranger than they must have looked in broad daylight.

The hot dogs were sort of rubbery on the outside, and resisted when you bit into them. Then your teeth went through the skin with a sort of *snap*, and juice squirted everywhere. The relish had a chemical taste and caused a funny sensation at the back of my throat.

I can't say they were really delicious hot dogs, but they were certainly different. Winston agreed. As soon as we finished our hot dogs, we both felt like burping a lot. These were not like the hot dogs in the square plastic-coated packages our mothers brought home, or like the hot dogs in the cafeteria at Genghis Khan. They were not like the hot dogs at the ballpark or anywhere else. Like them or not, Ed and Fred's red hots were unique.

As I said, Snark Street takes a bend to the left a little past Ed and Fred's. Winston Bongo had the idea that we could take a shortcut by turning up a side street that appeared to cut diagonally to the left, at a sharper angle, before Snark Street made its bend.

We turned left. In two minutes we were lost.

We had wandered into the strangest neighborhood I had ever seen. None of the streets ran parallel. Some of them turned this way and that; some just stopped short. Once we found ourselves in someone's backyard, and once in a funny alley that looked like it could have been in Paris, with cobblestones, and posters on the lampposts.

Everything in that neighborhood was all mixed together. There were little apartment buildings like the ones near Blueberry Park, and there were little frame houses that looked like farmhouses. Also, there were buildings I can only describe as weird, with skylights and carving all over them, and pieces of tile and stone and broken glass set into the cement to make all sorts of designs. And even though it was pretty late—maybe after 3:00 A.M.—lots of lights were on, and we could hear music playing in some of the buildings we passed. Looking into the lighted apartment windows, we saw all sorts of strange things—odd-looking plants, and weird paintings, and plaster busts sitting on pianos and windowsills.

It was by far the niftiest neighborhood I'd ever seen. We weren't even bothered by being lost. We just wandered around, looking at all the strange buildings and enjoying the place, burping and tasting our red-and-green hot dogs.

Some of the buildings had statues on the outside. It all reminded me of movies I had seen at the Snark Theater. It looked like some place in Europe. It was all very old-fashioned. The streets were narrow, and the streetlamps gave a yellow light—not white. I liked the place.

VI

Then, suddenly, we were back on Snark Street, a few blocks from our own neighborhood. "I never knew that neighborhood, the one we were just in, existed," I said.

"Neither did I," said Winston Bongo.

"It's quite a place," I said.

"Yes, interesting," Winston said.

We said good-bye in the street and sneaked into our respective apartment buildings. All in all, it had been one of the most unusual Snark Outs in my experience.

I was in bed by four-thirty and up at eight. At nine I was in school, fresh as a daisy.

In addition to Mrs. Macmillan's English class—where we are reading *Silas Marner*, easily the most boring book ever written—Winston Bongo and I are also in the same biology class. This is where we work on the idiotic biology notebooks. The biology teacher is Miss Sweet. She's about seventy years old. Miss Sweet doesn't speak to the class at all. Instead, she talks to the specimens, plants, and animals in the classroom.

"Oh, dear," Miss Sweet says, "why do they keep sending all these children here? How am I going to take care of my plants and animals properly if they keep sending these children here?" (She's saying this to various growing and living things.) She especially likes to talk to her alligator. This alligator is about two feet long and lives in a glass aquarium. Everyone in the class lives in hope that the alligator will bite Miss Sweet someday. She takes the thing out of its tank and cuddles it and coos to it. The class hopes the thing will bite her, not because Miss Sweet is hateful in herself—after all, it's obvious that she's crazy and not responsible—but just because such an event would break the horrible monotony.

Miss Sweet writes out a passage on the blackboard for us to copy into our biology notebooks.

On dewy mornings the spores separate from the parent plants. In some plants spores are not produced, but in others they are a prominent method of reproduction. As-xual spores are produced by division of one or more cells in a sporangium. In the blue-green algae zygotes are produced by the fusion of two gametes in the gametangium. Among the bryophytes and most of the pteridophytes the as-xual spores are called simply spores. In heterosporous plants (some pteridophytes and all spermatophytes) there are two kinds of as-xual spores, megaspores and microspores. . . .

Needless to say, none of us understand a word of this. It is sort of amusing that Miss Sweet always writes the word *sex* "s-x," but that's not enough to keep our minds alive. We have to copy all this down—it runs to two pages—and it has to be included in our notebooks.

I don't know what a spore is. No one has ever explained it to me. What's more, I don't care what a spore is, and I never want to learn. When I think of spores, I think of Miss Sweet's classroom, the smell of decaying vegetable matter and not-very-clean alligator tank, and thirty kids scratching away, copying pages for their biology notebooks.

Every so often, Miss Sweet asks if there's a boy in the class who has a driver's license. There's always an older kid who is repeating biology—someone who thought he could get away with not turning in a notebook with the correct number of pages. She asks that kid if he would mind being excused from school early and going to the garage to get her car. Naturally, the kid is delighted to do it. She tells him to bring the car around to the back entrance of Genghis Khan and park it there. The word will spread throughout the school, and there will be a huge crowd waiting to see Miss Sweet drive her car after school. Miss Sweet's car is a hot rod. It's an early Chevy, with a very shiny coat of black paint and a special suspension and those big tires in the back. No one knows how she came to have a car like that. It's usually in the shop for bodywork, except when she sends a kid to get it and park it behind the school.

The crowd is waiting when Miss Sweet gets behind the wheel and sends the car crunching into the nearest tree. She does this every time. I, personally, have seen Miss Sweet smash the front of her car twice since coming to Genghis Khan. After she crashes it and is led out of the car, a bit dazed and shaken, she goes into the school and calls the garage to come and tow it away and fix it.

I don't understand why someone doesn't come and take Miss Sweet away. It's so obvious that she's out of her mind. I feel sort of sorry for her, but like everyone else I wish that alligator would bite her once. I wonder why I feel that way when I really should just pity the poor old woman. I think I want it to happen because I believe that I'm suffering worse than she is, and it isn't fair.

I assume that somewhere there's a school in which the biology class doesn't consist of a bunch of miserable kids locked in a room with a poor old lunatic every day, but that school isn't Genghis Khan.

On this particular day—the day after our unusual Snark Out in that strange neighborhood—Winston Bongo appeared to be more depressed than usual. Most days, we managed to at least wink or make faces at each other while we copied the pages about spores, or whatever. Today, Winston looked terrible. He clawed at his sheet of notebook paper, trying to copy the gibberish Miss Sweet had written on the blackboard, with an expression like that of some kind of ape. Later he told me he didn't feel so well.

Winston Bongo had come down with German measles. He called me up that night to tell me. The doctor had been called, and he said that Winston would have to stay in bed for at least a week, and wouldn't be back in school for maybe ten days.

Of course, Snarking Out was out of the question for Winston, but what about me? Winston said that this was a good opportunity for me to rack up a few solo Snarks. For some time we had been Snarking Out at least twice a week. Before I had teamed up with him, Winston had made eleven solo Snarks. He knew that I had none to my credit, and, decently, instead of complaining about his own illness, he encouraged me to improve my record.

I considered the possibility that I might come down with German measles, too, hanging around with Winston as much as I did. But on checking with my mother, I found out that I had already had German measles when I was much younger. You can't get it twice.

I confess I was a little afraid at the prospect of Snarking on my own. Winston had always been the leader of our expeditions into the night, not only because he had originated the sport, but because he had Snarked alone. By encouraging me to take a Snark by myself, he was inviting me to become his equal. I thought that was nice of him.

"Be sure to call me and tell me about your next Snark," he said over the telephone.

I had no choice. I had to go through with it. Thinking

about it, I decided that there was nothing to be nervous about. After all, hadn't I Snarked many a time with good old Winston? There was nothing wrong with my technique. I would do it. What was more, I would make a really good job of it, have something really excellent to report to my friend. I would do something creative, something to expand the horizons of the gentlemanly sport of Snarking. I thought of our adventure the night before. I could do something in that interesting part of town. Then it came to me. I would make a speech in Blueberry Park!

VII

That night at supper, I found out a good deal about the neighborhood we'd visited the night before. My father knows Baconburg well. Once he worked part-time as a cab driver, and he prides himself on knowing every street in town and every section of town.

"What do you call that old-fashioned area down near where Snark Street bends west?" I asked him.

"That's the Old Town," he said. "Lots of artists and bohemians and odd people live there."

"I was walking around there last . . . weekend," I said. "It's really strange, the buildings and all."

"Lookit," my father said, "it's like this, Walter. When a

city gets started, it's not a city. Maybe it's just a few farms near each other, and maybe a store, and later a post office —a little village. If the village is in a good location, near a river, or a railroad, or what have you, it may grow up to be a town and later a city. By the time it's a city, there are people laying out the streets, and putting consecutive nubers on houses, and all of that. But what happens to the little village? In some cities, it gets demolished, or it burns down, or it just rots away. But sometimes, it just stays there, a little town or village in the middle of the modern city—like the pit in an avocado."

It was clever of him to work in that reference to an avocado. I think my father would be the happiest man in the world if I'd once try an avocado to see if I liked it. There's no chance of that happening, much as I'd like to make him proud of me.

"So that's why the twisty, narrow streets, and the houses that look like farmhouses?"

"They are farmhouses," my father said," and nearby is Blueberry Park. Did you know that people make speeches in Blueberry Park?"

"You told me all about that," I said. That was how I knew about it.

"It used to be quite the thing, when I was a boy, to go down there and make a speech," he said. "You know, people talk about all sorts of things there, from serious political speeches to pure raving and nonsense. The thing is, the audiences can be pretty rough. If you can't hold their attention, they'll break in with all sorts of wise remarks, hoots, and hollers. If you aren't careful, you can get a tomato flung at you."

"Did you ever make a speech there?" I asked.

"Oh, I suppose I did once or twice," my father said.

"What did you talk about?"

"Well, as a matter of fact, I spoke about misunderstood and unpopular vegetables," he said. "It was just too much of a temptation for that crowd. It was the middle of summer, and people had a lot of fruit with them. They ruined a sport jacket of mine."

From the things my father was saying, it seemed to me that I just *had* to make a speech in Blueberry Park. After all, he'd done it. I decided to Snark Out and do it that very night.

It was an unusually mild April. The weather was almost like June. Of course, it wouldn't have surprised me to wake up one morning and find it snowing. Baconburg weather is like that. But right now it was balmy and pleasant, and the air was sort of good-smelling. As Winston and I had seen, lots of people were staying up late, enjoying the pleasant night.

I'd Snark that night, and go straight to Blueberry Park and make a speech. The next day would be Saturday, and I'd go over to Winston Bongo's house and tell him all about it. They'd let me visit because I'd had German measles already.

I got to bed early again, prepared to Snark for all I was worth.

I woke up with a funny taste in my mouth. I was excited and a little frightened. I hated to admit to myself that I was chicken, but there it was. I was scared to go Snarking alone. Of course, I could have just gone back to sleep and forgotten about it, but then I'd have to admit to Winston Bongo, as well as to myself, that I didn't have the nerve.

Besides, I thought about my father making a speech at Blueberry Park. Probably he didn't sneak out of the house to do it, but he had done it. That was something else I was scared of. I had never made any kind of speech under any circumstances. Here I was going to make a speech after one in the morning in a place where I might get pelted with tomatoes.

The more I thought about it, the more I didn't like the idea—and the more certain it was that I had to go through with it.

I got dressed, and slipped out of the house in my usual smooth way. I didn't forget to take my stop watch—five minutes until I hit the street.

Of course, there was no Winston when I got there. I felt a little strange at first. The bus came along, and I got on. I sat in the back. All of this was pretty familiar to me. It wasn't so bad. I started to feel more comfortable. The only thing bothering me was the speech. I was a little uneasy about standing up and talking in front of people. I could have just stayed on the bus, gone to the Snark Theater, and seen a movie. That would constitute a good Snark for the record book. I didn't have to go through with this speech bit.

But I did. I just wasn't willing to do an ordinary Snark as my very first solo. Winston Bongo had invented the activity and would be remembered in history for his great deed. I wanted to do something great, too. I wanted to contribute something to Snarking as a worldwide cultural activity. I was realizing that I wasn't content to be just a follower. I was out to do something to astound Winston Bongo—and generations of Snarkers who would come after us.

I got off the bus across the street from Blueberry Park.

I marched right up to the place where the speaker had been carrying on the night before. The crowd was standing around, listening to three different speakers. The three speakers were standing on top of the one-foot wall that surrounds the park. They were maybe fifteen feet apart and all going at once, full blast. At the back of the crowd, you could drift from one speaker to another by sort of moving along sideways.

Of course, the people in the crowd were answering the speakers, arguing with them and heckling them. Some of the hecklers, situated between two speakers, were able to answer back to two speakers, one after the other.

I wandered back and forth at the back of the crowd, picking up one speech and then another.

First speaker:	Brothers and sisters, God doesn't want us to eat meat! It is against nature's plan!
Shouts from the crowd:	Tell that to my dog!
	Didn't I see you at Burger King an hour ago?
	Listen to him! Listen to him! He's right, I tell you.
Second speaker:	Colonial rule must end! The British have broken too many promises for too long. I say get the British

out of Kenya, East Africa, today!

Shouts from the crowd: Yaaay! Get those British out of Kenya!

Idiot! The British have been out of Kenya for years!

Don't eat meat! Don't eat meat!

Third speaker: *Whoop! Huhn! Huhn! Huhn! Eeeeeeeek!* Wow! The devil. *Woooo!* The dev-vill! Dee dev-v-vil-l-l! *Eeeeek!* The devil gonna get us! *Whoooooo!*

Shouts from the crowd: Right on, brother. Tell 'em! He's telling it like it is.

It's all because of those British. They did it!

Don't eat meat! Don't eat meat!

First speaker: I never ate a hamburger in my life!

Shouts from the crowd: It's the devil! He's right! It's the devil!

Second speaker:	They did it in Ireland! They did it in India!
Shouts from the crowd:	War! War with England. We beat them twice already—we can do it again!
Third speaker:	*Hooo! Hooo! Hooo! Humma, humma humma! Goo!*
Shouts from the crowd:	He eats meat! That's why he can't make sense! The devil made him eat a hamburger!
First speaker:	God says . . .
Second speaker:	Get the British . . .
Third speaker:	The devil's got me! *Ooooooh!*
First speaker:	Whole grains . . .
Second speaker:	Jomo Kenyatta . . .
Third speaker:	*Eeeeeek!*
First speaker:	. . . makes you sexually impotent . . .
Second speaker:	. . . agents after me . . .
Third speaker:	. . . devil after me . . .
First speaker:	. . . food companies after me . . .
Shouts from the crowd:	Right! Wrong! Shut up! Go! Stop! *Wheeee!*

VIII

The third speaker—the one talking about the devil—was the crowd's favorite. Mine, too. He wound up his speech by leaping into the air, waving his arms around, twisting, trembling, screaming, and kicking. He was really a good public speaker. He knew how to hold your attention, and he was obviously sincere. Even the don't-eat-meat guy and the free-Kenya-East-Africa guy stopped speaking and turned to watch and listen to the end of the devil's-gonna-get-you guy's speech.

At the very end, he threw himself high into the air and was caught, as he fell, by a number of people in the audience. They carried him away. I guess they were friends of his.

The other two speakers finished up, too—but nothing like the devil guy—and stepped off the wall to the cheers and boos of the crowd. Then two other speakers got started. One was a person who believed that animals should wear clothing. The other was a person who said that beings from other planets were putting stuff in our food to make us stupid. The crowd liked him. "It's working," someone shouted, "look at you!"

Gradually, I had edged my way up to the front of the crowd. I was having a good time. It was interesting to listen to the various speakers and observe their styles. They weren't all speakers, to be precise. One old lady played the harmonica, and another guy whistled. He didn't last very long.

I had sort of forgotten about my intention to make a speech myself. I was just enjoying myself, listening to the other speakers and the comments from the audience. If I had given it any thought, I might have told myself that I would just watch and listen tonight and see how it was done. Then I'd come back another night and make a speech myself.

Just being in Blueberry Park and listening to the others was enough to constitute a very respectable Snark, one I could report to Winston Bongo about. He'd be sure to be interested in the "devil" guy—I was planning to do a good imitation of him for my friend.

In other words, I was chickening out.

Then, right in front of me, the person giving a speech on how eating raw zucchini cures cancer came to the end. "Well, that's all I have to say," she said. "Who's next? You?" She was looking right at me.

The next thing I knew, the old zucchini lady had hopped down off the wall. I felt a sort of stirring in the little crowd of listeners behind me. Somehow I got up on the wall and faced them.

Only at that moment did I realize that I didn't have anything to talk about. I had been thinking about getting up the nerve to give a speech at all—I hadn't really pictured myself saying anything. For a second, I considered trying an imitation of the "devil" guy, but this crowd had just heard him, and I was pretty sure I couldn't bring it off in front of strangers.

I must have just stood there for a few seconds, because somebody shouted, "Well, let's hear it, pal!"

"I'm just a kid," I shouted back. I was going to say something about being just a kid, and would the people please let me off and not holler things at me. If I'd gotten all that out, I have no doubt they would have heckled me right out of the park. As it happened, I didn't get to finish my creepy cop-out beginning because someone shouted, "That's interesting." Another voice said, "I thought he was a streetcar!"

It wasn't really bad-natured, the heckling and shouts from the audience. In fact, those shouts sort of made me feel more comfortable.

"I'm just a high-school kid," I shouted back, "and that means I'm supposed to be getting educated."

"So?" a voice from the crowd asked.

"So I'm not, that's all," I said. "I'm not getting educated, and nobody else in my school is getting educated."

"That's because you're all lazy bums!" someone shouted.

"No, we're not!" I said. "If we lose interest, whose fault is it? I'm interested in the things people say here. How come I've never heard a word in Genghis Khan High School that made me want to stay awake for whatever comes next?"

"You kids are all on drugs!" shouted a voice. "You eat meat—that's what's wrong with you, sonny," shouted another.

"What's wrong with me," I said, "is that my school is part garbage can and part loony bin. My biology teacher is about a hundred years old and talks to things that can't answer back. My English teacher is a full-time professional

Jew-hater. My math teacher is always falling asleep in the classroom. My history teacher talks about nothing but his personal problems, and the gym teacher is some kind of homicidal maniac! That's what's wrong with me! I'm growing up ignorant, and I don't particularly want to!"

"Tell 'em, kid!" someone shouted. "That's good! That's good!" someone else said. "You poor kid, you're gonna grow up an idjit!" another member of the audience said. "Those meat-eating teachers! Those dirty meat eaters! I'll kill 'em!" someone was shrieking.

"Who allows those bozos to be teachers?" I shouted. "Look, maybe I'm a dope. Maybe I can't learn anything."

"You're no dope, kid!" I heard from the crowd. "Naw, he's real smart, I can tell," someone else said.

"Maybe I am a dope," I went on, "but how am I ever going to find out if I'm a dope or not? How can I find out if I can handle high school if nobody wants to teach me anything?"

"The kid's right!"

"It's a shame, those lousy bum teachers!"

"They're making stoopids out of our young kids!"

"Kill the meat eaters! Kill the meat eaters!"

I was a big success.

I didn't have a good ending for my speech, and I didn't have any actual suggestions about what could be done. Basically, my speech consisted of my saying "school stinks," and the audience more or less agreeing with me.

As soon as I was finished, I realized that, had I thought of it, I would have liked to end on a high note and jump off the wall to the loud cheers of my listeners. Instead, I just sort of petered out. "Well, that's all, I guess," I said and stepped down. There was some weak cheering, and one or two people patted me on the back, but most of the crowd was already listening to the next speaker.

"The government is ruining our feet!" he shouted.
"Tell 'em! Tell 'em!"
"Right on!"
"They ruined my brother's feet!"
"Eat meat and ruin your feet!"
"Whoopee!"

I made my way to the back of the crowd.

IX

I moved away from the park. I checked my watch: 2:10 A.M. My first solo Snark was a complete success, so far.

My next stop was Ed and Fred's Red Hots. I ordered one with everything and extra onions. There was someone else in the place, eating a hot dog under the yellow lights. It was a kid, a girl, a little taller than me, with a pointy rat nose and pimples. She had short blonde hair, tinged with green and sticking out in all directions. She was wearing a baggy red skirt that came below her knees and black, pointy shoes. She had skinny legs. She was also wearing a jacket about five sizes too big for her. It was orange and light blue. CUSTER, it said on the back in white letters.

"You go to Genghis Khan," Rat Face said.

I must have given her a look that said, "Do I know you?" or, "How do you know where I go to school?"

"I heard your speech," Rat Face said. "I go to George Armstrong Custer."

"Good school," I said.

"It's a toilet," Rat Face said. "You want a root beer?"

"Uh, sure, thanks," I said.

Rat Face went to the counter and got two small root beers. "What you said was good," she said.

"Thanks," I said. I wasn't too comfortable with this girl. She looked sort of sinister. I would have bet she had a knife on her.

"You ever go to the Snark?" she asked.

That took me by surprise. "Sure," I said. "Sometimes."

"You sneak out of the house when your parents are asleep?"

"That's right." This was really amazing. This was going to be a bigger part of my report than the speech I'd given. Winston Bongo was going to be as amazed as I was. It looked like I'd run into a natural Snarker.

"I would have gone there tonight," Rat Face said, "but they're showing two movies by this Italian guy, Visconti. *The Earth Trembles* and something else. I hate his stuff. I'm not about to pay half a dollar to watch some guys packing anchovies for two hours."

"Yeah," I said. I wondered how long this girl had been Snarking. She seemed to know a lot about movies.

"Now, next week there's the James Dean Festival. Aaah!"

"Yeah," I said.

"My name's Bentley Saunders Harrison Matthews," Rat Face said.

"I'm Walter Galt," I said.

"The kids call me Rat," she said.

"No kidding," I said.

"You can call me Rat."

"OK," I said. Bentley Saunders Harrison Matthews had an oversized comb sticking out of her pocket. A couple of times she ran the comb through her spiky blonde-green hair. The comb was bright pink.

"Uh, Rat, have you been Snarking . . . I mean, going to the Snark at night for very long?"

"Years, pal, years."

This was amazing. If this kid was telling the truth, she was possibly the world's champion Snarker. "Do any other kids from George Armstrong Custer do it?"

"Snark Out?" She used the same term! Incredible! "No, the kids at Custer are mostly insects, mentally. Some of the boys are not too bad—the ones I take automotive shop with, for instance—but they've been brainwashed to hate me. The girls are all subnerds. They fear me because I am a liberated woman. I ignore them. They get their kicks spreading rumors about me."

"Yeah, the kids at Genghis Khan are mostly subnerds, too." I liked that expression. It was the first time I'd heard it.

When Rat was telling me about the kids at George Armstrong Custer, she shoved her hands deep into the pockets of her too-large jacket and hunched her shoulders. She had a habit of bending her ankles so the soles of her shoes faced each other and standing on the sides of her feet. She was sort of cute, in a horrible way.

"Yeah . . . well," Rat said. "I'm not usually too friendly. I just wanted to say that I liked your speech."

"Yeah . . . well," I said.

"Yeah."

"Well."

"Yeah, well, maybe I'll see you at the Snark sometime," Rat said.

"Hey, yeah . . . well."

"Yeah, well, so long." Rat turned and hunched her shoulders a couple of times and walked out of the glassed-in, yellow-lighted enclosure in front of Ed and Fred's Red Hots.

X

The next day in school was mostly standard. There was only one event that I would have to report to Winston Bongo when I saw him that afternoon. Miss Sweet went around the classroom, passing out pairs of scissors, those lightweight, blunt-nosed things we used to get in first grade for doing paper cutouts. Then she came around with a big black can—like a paint can—and a pair of tongs. Reaching into the can with the tongs, she deposited a large, formaldehyde-soaked frog on the table in front of each kid.

"Cut them up, now! Cut them up!" she said to us.

I think it would be best to draw a curtain over what

then took place in the biology class. I will just say that I was not the only one to throw up.

Winston Bongo was delighted when I told him about the dissection lesson. I told him he might not have liked it so much if he had been there.

Then I went on to tell him about my triumph at Blueberry Park. He was impressed, as I knew he would be. He made me give my speech, as well as I could remember it, a couple of times. I also had to tell him what everybody else said. Winston said that for a first-ever solo Snark I had exhibited real genius. I was flattered. I knew that my friend did not pay compliments lightly.

I was saving Bentley Saunders Harrison Matthews, also known as Rat, for my big ending. When I described her and told Winston all about our conversation, he got so excited that I was scared I might have caused him to take a turn for the worse in his recovery.

"Do you realize what this means?" he sputtered. "We haven't been alone all this time! Who knows how many other Snarkers may exist! I never expected anything like this! We have to meet this Rat again and talk to her. Maybe she is in touch with other Snarkers. This could turn out to be a vast worldwide movement."

"I don't think she knows any other Snarkers," I said. "She's sort of antisocial."

"Just the same," Winston said, "She's a great genius. Look, she's invented Snarking Out all on her own. That makes her as great a creative being as . . . myself."

Winston Bongo was all for Snarking Out together that very night. I had a hard time convincing him that he was still sick, and had better stay in bed.

"Well, I'm going to get better in a hurry," he said. "I had planned to stay sick until the first day of Easter vacation, but this is too important."

Meanwhile, Winston made me promise to Snark Out as often as possible, and to look for Bentley Saunders Harrison Matthews in the Snark Theater, and, if possible, to bring her to see Winston.

I promised I would do that. I also promised to visit Winston every day, or call him on the telephone, and to bring him the pages of the biology notebook to copy. Also, I was to bring him the history notebook, which was pretty much the same as the biology notebook, and the social-studies notebook, which was different in that you had to find certain newspaper articles, cut them out, and paste them in. You didn't have to read them—just cut them out and paste them in, and hand in the notebook at the end of the year. All of Genghis Khan High School works on the notebook system. Our English notebook consisted of book reports, which were mostly written about movies we'd seen based on books. If we hadn't been regular moviegoers, we would have had to copy our book reports off the flaps of books like the other kids, but we liked our way better. Not that Mrs. Macmillan ever read the reports; she graded by weight, like the other teachers. The most any of the teachers would ever do would be to open a notebook at random and read part of a page. If this happened with, say, a history notebook, and the teacher found out that the page was your older sister's English homework from five years ago, it might go badly with you.

One of the tricks kids use in preparing nice, heavy notebooks is this: You take your actual, say, biology notes, maybe twenty-five pages' worth. Then you take twenty-five pages of just anything with writing, and shave a quarter of an inch off the outside edge of the page. You put a genuine page, then a shaved-down fake page, then a genuine page, and so on. This way you have a fifty-page notebook, a certain A. When the teacher flips the pages, the book will always open to a real biology assignment. When you've gotten your A, you can take apart the biology notebook and use some of the contents for your social-studies notebook.

Another thing you can do is obtain someone's last-year's notebook cover that got an A. You erase the grade and use it again. The theory is that if Miss Sweet liked the picture last year, she'll like it again this year. I know of a cover with a picture of Liberace on it with labels indicating eyes, teeth, nose, hair, etc., that has gotten five A's already, and, having paid three dollars for it, I have it in my drawer ready to get its sixth grade.

I could probably make my own cover and get an A with it, but it's more challenging to cheat. At least this way, we're actually learning some skills. And the teachers are cheating. The whole reason for the notebook system is so that if anyone accused them of never teaching anything, they could grab one of the notebooks and say, "Look, this kid knows all about sports and grasshoppers and all this stuff—how can you accuse me of never doing my job?"

I solo Snarked a couple of times during Winston Bongo's illness. I didn't go back to Blueberry Park. I wanted to polish up my speaking technique, but I thought it would be more fun to do that when Winston was along.

Instead, I went to the Snark Theater. I saw two good double features—*Alexander Nevsky*, an exciting Russian movie, and *Kiss Me Deadly*, a detective movie. Also I saw *Frankenstein* and Walt Disney's *Song of the South*.

I didn't see Bentley Saunders Harrison Matthews, *aka* Rat, although I looked for her. I was pretty sure she'd turn up at the James Dean Festival, since she'd mentioned it, and I planned to be there, looking for her.

XI

·Winston got better. To celebrate, we Snarked Out and saw *The Mask of Fu Manchu* and *Mutiny on the Bounty* (the original version, with Charles Laughton and Clark Gable). We kept a sharp eye out for Bentley Saunders Harrison Matthews, but we didn't see her.

Easter vacation started, and with it the James Dean Festival. Every night the Snark Theater was showing a James Dean film, along with something else. The first night they had *Rebel Without a Cause* and *Attack of the Mayan Mummy*.

As we were watching the James Dean movie, I felt a sharp poke in the ribs. I looked over to my left and there was a skinny, angular figure. It was Rat, also known as Bentley Saunders Harrison Matthews.

"Hiya, Walter," Rat said. "Great stuff, huh?"

Rat was obviously a great fan of James Dean. She was all excited by his appearance on the screen and continually nudged me, pointed at the screen, and whistled, panted, moaned, sobbed, and made comments about James Dean's looks. At times, various members of the audience tried to hush Rat, but she would not be quiet.

"Leave me alone," she said. "Just because you can't appreciate a great actor is no reason I can't have a good time."

The James Dean movie ended—Rat cheered loudly—and *The Attack of the Mayan Mummy* came on. Almost at once, people began fidgeting, talking, and leaving. As the movie progressed, those people still in the theater were almost all engaged in conversation in normal tones of voice. People lit up cigarettes, friends called to each other, and someone behind me was humming and drumming on the top of the empty seat in front of him. Nobody complained. It wasn't the sort of movie you'd want to pay close attention to.

Rat had come up with a chrome cigarette holder about two feet long, and was smoking a black cigarette with a gold tip on it. There's no smoking in the Snark Theater, but people smoke anyway. If the usher has nothing to do, he'll tell you to quit smoking, but since he's usually got a cigarette in his mouth, nobody pays too much attention to him.

"This your friend?" Rat asked, pointing at Winston with the hot cigarette end.

I introduced the two Snarkers. It was a historic moment —two great pioneers in the same field meeting for the first time.

51

"Walter has told me a lot about you," Winston said. "I understand you've done a lot of Snarking Out."

"If you mean coming to the movies late at night, I've been doing that for a couple of years," Rat said.

"Would you say that you've averaged a Snark a week, or what?" Winston wanted to know.

"I come here on the average three times a week," Rat said. "Some weeks, when I'm bored, or when they've got movies I particularly want to see, I'll come here every night."

"Wow!" Winston Bongo said. "That means you've got the greatest Snarking record of anybody probably."

"Record, schmecord," Rat said. "I've got bigger fish to fry than counting how many times I go to the movies. Besides, if you're interested in records, you'll be interested in meeting my Uncle Flipping."

"Your Uncle Flipping?" I asked.

"Yes, my uncle, Flipping Hades Terwilliger," Rat said. "He's been coming here every night for fifteen or twenty years. He's probably here now. I'll call him."

Rat made a trumpet of her hands and bellowed out, "Hey, Uncle Flipping! You here?" Nobody objected. *The Attack of the Mayan Mummy* unreeled on the screen with nobody watching. In the row in front of us, two guys were unwrapping an elaborate picnic and arranging all sorts of food on a tablecloth they'd spread across their knees."

"That you, niece?" a voice called from way down in the first row.

"Uncle Flipping!" Rat shouted.

"Keep calling, I'll find you by your voice," Uncle Flipping called out. In a short while, we were joined by a man in a suit with all the buttons buttoned, a tight white collar and tie, and one of those straw hats you hardly see anymore.

Rat introduced us to her uncle. Uncle Flipping also appeared to know the guys with the picnic. They offered him a pickle, which he accepted and munched while he talked to us, half sitting, half leaning on a seat back in the row in front of us.

"These guys are interested in how many times you've come to this movie house in the middle of the night," Rat said.

"Let's see," Uncle Flipping said. "Every night for seventeen years—that's um, six thousand two hundred and five as of a couple of months ago. Add sixty—no, fifty-eight—that's six thousand two hundred sixty-three times. Six thousand two hundred sixty-three, that's it."

"Holy God," Winston Bongo said.

I knew what Winston Bongo was feeling. He was like some guy in the mountains of California, or some other primitive place, who invents the steam engine all by himself—spends years doing it. Then, when he's got it perfected, he comes down out of the mountains and finds out that it was already invented in 1543 by Blasco De Garay. Here was Winston, who had just gotten used to the idea that maybe Rat had done more Snarking than we had, and suddenly he meets Rat's uncle, who has come to the Snark Theater more than six thousand times. Of course, Winston was probably thinking, it isn't the same for an adult who doesn't have to sneak out of the house without waking anybody up.

"You understand," Uncle Flipping was saying, "that since I live with my brother-in-law, Saunders II—Bentley's father—and his family, I always have to sneak out to come here. Otherwise, I'd be waking up the whole house every night."

Winston Bongo was a broken man. It meant more to him than it did to me. I must say, I always Snarked more for the sport of it than to build up a world record, but Winston, as the inventor (he thought) of Snarking, was very concerned with how history would regard him. Now he realized that it wouldn't even mention him.

"Say, Rat Face," Uncle Flipping said. "Why don't you invite your friends home for breakfast? I believe it's the spring vacation, is it not?"

"Sure," Rat said. "You guys want to have breakfast at my house?"

"We'll have to go home and leave notes for our parents, indicating that we've gotten up extra early to go over to see a friend," I said. It occurred to me that this would be a new Snarking wrinkle—sneaking out in the middle of the night, then sneaking back in the wee hours of the morning to leave a note representing us as having snuck out some hours later, and then sneaking out again. It was very sophisticated. I was going to mention this new departure to Winston, but I thought it might depress him just then.

"I'll go along with you guys and wait outside while you write the notes," Rat said.

"I'm going to stay here and watch the James Dean movie again," Uncle Flipping said. "I'll see you all at breakfast."

XII

         Rat waited in the street while Winston and I sneaked into our respective apartments. Once inside, I removed the pillows and things from the bed and arranged it as though I had been sleeping in it. Then I wrote a note:

> Dear Mom and Dad,
> I forgot to tell you last night. I have
> to get up extra, extra early to meet
> Winston Bongo. We're going to have
> breakfast at a friend's house. See
> you later.
>
>   Love,
>   Walter

    I taped the note to my bedroom door. I didn't expect it to arouse any curiosity. I had my parents trained to accept my irregular hours. Even when I didn't plan any Snarking adventures, I made a point of going to bed and getting up at all sorts of different times. Sometimes, when I had come home from a late Snark, I wouldn't go to bed at all—I'd just pretend that I'd been up since dawn and give my parents a cheerful good morning when they woke up. I don't have any trouble staying up all night. I just get to bed early the next night and catch up on sleep.

I met Rat and Winston in the street, "We can walk to my house." Rat said. "We've got plenty of time before breakfast. It isn't even dawn yet."

We began to walk. Winston appeared to have pulled himself together. It was obvious that he was going to have to give up his idea of being known as the Father of Snarking. I assumed he would just have to find another career. I must say, he was being a good sport about it.

Rat had a lot to say as we walked. It turned out that in addition to movies she had any number of interests. One of the things she talked about was poisonous snakes, which interested her. She knew a lot about them. Her favorite was something called the Gaboon viper. She said that the bite it could give was a doozy. She also said that she wanted to go out West and participate in a rattlesnake roundup. Apparently in some places out West, people go to areas where rattlesnakes are known to hang out in great numbers, and they catch scads of them. Then they have a big hoop-de-do and give prizes for the biggest snake caught, the most snakes caught, and the rarest snake caught. They also fry up a lot of rattlesnakes and eat them. It all sounded horrible.

"You don't have any snakes at home?" I asked Rat. Since I was going to her house, I wanted to know if I ought to be prepared for anything.

"Not at present," Rat said. That was all I wanted to know. I can live without snakes—and I plan to.

Rat was pretty outspoken. She had a lot of things to say

about James Dean and the things she would have been willing to do with him, and with no one else, if only he had not died. Winston and I got the impression that Rat knew a lot more about sex than we did, so we kept off the subject in order not to appear ignorant.

Another enthusiasm of Rat's was cars. She told us the make and year of various parked cars we passed. After a while, I wished she'd get back onto sex. For an antisocial kid, Rat certainly tended to chatter on once she got going.

And Rat told us about how it was at George Armstrong Custer High School. It seems that Custer High works on the notebook system, like Genghis Khan. Rat told us about some of the teachers there, and we told her about ours. Rat admitted that our Miss Sweet was, by far, crazier than any of the teachers at George Armstrong Custer. About the most distinguished teacher they had appeared to be this guy who weighed about four hundred and fifty pounds and wore a wig. That's picturesque, but it can't compete with an old lady who talks to plants.

We were walking in the direction of the Old Town. It seemed that was where Rat's house was. I was glad to have the opportunity to do some more exploring in that neighborhood. It was sufficiently late for almost all the lights in the houses to be out. The night was very mild. We talked quietly as we walked through the narrow, crooked streets.

We came to a stretch of pavement with an old iron fence running alongside of it. Heavy vines—creepers, I think they're called—had grown up and around the iron bars. Even though it was still too early in the spring for the vines to have leaves, they were so thick that it was impossible to see what was beyond the fence. I was reminded of haunted houses in movies. I imagined that there was a strange old mansion behind the overgrown fence.

We came to the gate. It had iron curlicues along the top. Attached to the gate was a little sign, flaking enamel on rusty metal, that said NO VISITORS.

"Here we are," Rat said. This was where she lived! I was only half surprised. She pushed the gate open. It squeaked, as I knew it would. It was just beginning to be light—not quite dawn, just a little before dawn. I could just make out the strange old house on the grounds behind the iron gate. It was just the sort of house I expected.

"Keep quiet," Rat said, "everybody's still asleep. We'll go to my soundproof room."

I admit to having been a little bit scared.

XIII

Rat unlocked the front door. Winston Bongo whispered to me, "I tell you, this house could be in a horror movie."

I agreed with him. The house had lots of towers and chimneys poking up out of it, and there were shutters hanging crookedly next to the windows.

The key Rat used to unlock the door was one of those big, old-fashioned ones about four inches long with fancy curlicues on the end. "Now, don't make any noise," she said. "Just follow me."

The inside of the house was just as weird as the outside. We were in some sort of entrance hall. There was a bunch of old-fashioned furniture, a worn-out carpet, and a big statue of what appeared to be a tall, skinny chicken. I could see what was in the hall, because there was a dim lamp making long, dark shadows everywhere.

We followed Rat to a door in the side of the staircase. She flipped a switch and a light came on, revealing some stairs going down. The stairs led to a basement. "Now *this* is my soundproof room," Rat said proudly, opening a door.

Rat's soundproof room was fairly large. It had thick carpeting on the floor and three or four thicknesses of carpet nailed to the inside of the door. There were heavy drapes on the walls, and squares of cork covered the ceiling. It was very quiet in there. I could hear myself breathe.

"You could shoot off a cannon in here and nobody upstairs would hear a thing," Rat said.

There were a few articles of overstuffed furniture in the room, and a huge wooden cabinet that looked like a stereo speaker, but it was much too big for that. On a table there was some powerful-looking, old-fashioned electronic stuff. I couldn't tell what it was.

"This is my hi-fi," Rat said. "I'll bet you guys have never seen anything like this. My Uncle Flipping put this together about thirty years ago. In those days, they really knew something about sound. My father helped me fix up this soundproof room when Uncle Flipping gave me all this equipment. Behind the drapes there's twelve inches of fiberglass batting, and the walls and floor are floating on rubber mountings. There's an electric fan that goes on with the lights to change the air, or it would get plenty stuffy in here."

"Is that the speaker?" I asked.

"That is the Klugwallah 850-ohm Sound Reproducing System," Rat said, "and this is a custom-built amplifier. Don't stand too near it when I turn it on; it can electrocute you at a distance of a foot on a humid night. This, here," Rat said, indicating another giant piece of wooden furniture, "is a free-standing Fluchtzbesser turntable. Inside that wooden cabinet is an eleven-hundred-pound piece of granite. Yes, sir, this is about the finest hi-fi ever assembled in the city of Baconburg."

"And it only has the one speaker?" Winston Bongo asked.

Rat gave Winston a sideways look. "Stereo is for sissies," she said.

Naturally we wanted to hear Rat's hi-fi. She flipped a bunch of switches on the amplifier. It was basically a big, black metal box, about the size of an air conditioner, with gigantic blackened tubes sticking out of the top. Various red lights came on when Rat flipped the switches, and there was a low buzzing, humming sound in the room.

"Just give the tubes a minute to warm up," Rat said. "You guys like Scallion?"

A pale blue aura of light appeared around the amplifier. Rat went to a shelf to get a Scallion album. Scallion is a rock group. They are famous for giving very creative performances. For example, they have a 35-foot-deep glass tank filled with water on stage with them. At one point in their concert, they all get into a diving bell, and it gets lowered into the tank. Then they play a number underwater. After that, the members of the band each come out an escape hatch and swim to the surface, playing and singing. Sometimes they take members of the audience captive and hold them for ransom. They won't give them back until they get a thousand dollars for each hostage.

They also wrestle a live gorilla onstage. Then they get run over by a United Parcel Service truck. For a finale, they set fire to an eighteen-foot-tall papier-maché mastodon. It's sort of their trademark.

Scallion all wear galvanized-iron suits. While they're somewhat more conservative than a lot of rock bands, musically they're considered OK. Besides that, they have a very good philosophy, which they express in their songs. For example, some of their popular songs include: "I'm Not Hurting Anybody, Why Don't You Leave Me Alone?"; "Everybody Is Against Me"; "Unhip People Are Jerks"; "I'm Neat"; "The System Stinks"; and "Human Beings All Gotta Be Like Me or I'll Kill Them." Their biggest hit is "Drool on Me."

I, personally, am not much in favor of rock music, being more of a Mozart fan, but many kids like Scallion a lot. Another feature of that band is that they don't actually sing. They sort of shout, scream, and gurgle, mumble, hum, and whistle.

Rat put a Scallion record on the Fluchtzbesser turntable and lowered the tone arm. What then followed was one of the strangest experiences I've ever had. The sound was so powerful, so intense, that I couldn't stay on my feet. My knees went rubbery, and I had to sort of crawl over to one of the overstuffed chairs. I noticed that Winston Bongo had a very strange expression and seemed to be gasping for breath. He looked like he was in pain. I know I was.

Once I got to the chair and managed to crawl into it, I felt my body being blasted into the cushions by the sound waves from the Klugwallah Sound Reproducing System. It felt as though I was facing into a strong wind—a hurricane, in fact—but it wasn't a wind, it was just wave after wave of vibrations blaring out of the speaker. I couldn't hear anything like music, even Scallion-style. I did hear various things popping and snapping inside my head. I was scared that my eardrums might be bursting.

Through all this, Rat was hopping around, snapping her fingers, and slapping her knees. At one point, she put her mouth close to my ear and shouted something. I couldn't make out what she was saying. I think it was something like "Great midrange tones, huh?"

Winston Bongo was making weak motions with his hands. He was trying to get Rat to turn the thing off. It took awhile, but finally Rat stopped cavorting around and noticed Winston's feeble motions. She switched off the deadly hi-fi.

Winston was sweating. "You little creep," he gasped, "how could you do such a thing? When I get my strength back, I'm going to kill you."

I was amazed at the silence in the room. I was also grateful that I was still alive and could hear. I hadn't gotten around to being mad at Rat for doing that to us, but I could see Winston's point. For a second, I considered punching Rat in the head.

"Oh, you don't like rock? Why didn't you say so? I just

keep that record around because it shows off the hi-fi. I think Scallion is sort of juvenile myself. Here, I'll put on some really good sounds for you." Rat got out a stack of records. When she put the first one on, Winston and I flinched, but she had turned down the volume to no more than an ear-splitting roar. Rat treated us to a concert of obscure rock groups, including Eevo, Weevo, Geevo, So-Silly Boodi, Ken and the Maniacs, and Thug.

It could have been worse. Rat could have been a disco fan, which, in combination with the Klugwallah-Fluchtzbesser, might have been fatal.

Rat switched off the custom monster amplifier. "It must be broad daylight by now," she said. "Let's go up and meet the family and have some breakfast."

XIV

We followed Rat upstairs. In the hall, I saw that what I had taken for a statue of a tall, skinny chicken was, in fact, just that. It was carved out of wood and still had some old gold paint sticking to it. Rat told us that the statue was a souvenir her grandfather had brought back from a trip. It seems that Rat's grandfather is a world traveler, always going to some weird place or other.

"As a matter of fact, we don't know exactly where my grandfather is right now," Rat said. "Last we heard of him he had boarded an Icelandic steamer, the *Pippicksdottir*, in Port Newark, New Jersey. He started the family business. Now he just travels. My father and Uncle Flipping run the business now."

"What business is that?" Winston Bongo asked.

"Our family owns Bullfrog Industries," Rat said. "Surely you're familiar with Bullfrog Root Beer? It used to be the most popular soft drink around here, more popular than Moxie, Killer Cola, and Doctor Feldman's Banana Tonic. It still sells quite a bit in certain parts of the country. Grandfather got the recipe from an old baba in the forests of Nepal."

"I've never heard of it," I said.

"Well, you'll have some with breakfast," Rat said. "We drink gallons of the stuff around here. Anyway, Bullfrog Industries does a lot more than make root beer now. The root beer was just the first product. Now our family company makes Bullfrog Glue, Bullfrog Yoghurt, Bullfrog Tennis Shoes and Sneakers, Bullfrog Rubber Bands and Office Supplies, and Bullfrog Space Technology Products. They all have the same secret ingredient that makes Bullfrog Root Beer the best."

"What's the secret ingredient?" Winston Bongo asked.

"I can't tell you. It's a secret," Rat said, "but I'll give you a hint: It hops, croaks, and eats flies."

Naturally, we thought she was kidding.

Through a large pair of glass doors we could see a bunch of people doing something in the garden. We sort of recognized Uncle Flipping; we had only seen him in the dark-

ness of the Snark. There were also some other people—
Rat's family, we supposed. They were being led in some
sort of exercises or calisthenics by a fellow in a long silk
robe with flowers and dragons embroidered on it.

"That's Heinz, our Chinese butler," Rat said. "He leads
the family exercises every morning before breakfast. I
usually don't do them."

The only thing that was Chinese about Heinz was his
robe. He had blue eyes, blond hair, a large, straight nose,
and a pink complexion. Heinz was going through some
strange slow-moving exercise that involved striking all
sorts of uncomfortable-looking poses, waving his arms and
standing on one foot. When he stood on one foot, we
could see that he was wearing high-topped basketball
shoes. The others, two men and two women, were wearing
bathrobes, pajamas, and nightgowns. They appeared to be
trying to imitate or follow the movements Heinz was making. None of them seemed to be able to do it. They were
all moving every which way, waving their arms, wobbling
on one foot, crouching, stretching, and jumping into the
air.

The family finished their exercises and filed into the
house. Rat introduced us to everybody. There was her father, Saunders Harrison Matthews II, her mother, Minna
Terwilliger Matthews, Uncle Flipping Hades Terwilliger,
whom we had already met, and Aunt Terwilliger. Aunt
Terwilliger was about six feet tall and skinny, and everybody called her Aunt Terwilliger.

Heinz, the butler, bowed low and said, "Please call me
F'ang Tao Sheh." Everybody called him Heinz.

After we had all been introduced, Saunders Harrison

Matthews II, Rat's father, said, "It's a pleasure to meet some of Rat's friends. Especially since you don't have hair dyed pink and strange clothing like some of the other people she's brought home."

We all went into the dining room. It was a nice room with lots of windows and a long table. Everybody sat down, and Heinz served breakfast. It was an unusual breakfast. We had Chinese gooseberries, which I had never seen before. They're fuzzy brown on the outside, and about the size of an egg. Inside they're green and taste somewhere between a banana and a lime. I liked them. We also had homemade crunchy granola with little tiny orange slices, corn-meal bagels, Uncle Flipping's special high-protein drink, which was like a gritty milk shake, and Bullfrog Root Beer, which was served hot in cups or in glasses with ice. The older people had theirs hot—Rat, Winston, and I had ours cold.

Everybody ate in silence until the Bullfrog Root Beer was served. Then the conversation at the table got started. Aunt Terwilliger began by making a sort of speech about grand opera. She was against it. Later, Rat told us that her aunt had just about every opera recording ever made. Her aunt spent hours in her bedroom every day listening to them, but all the rest of her time was spent arguing that people shouldn't listen to operas, and, above all, they shouldn't go to see them performed. Rat said that Aunt Terwilliger makes regular appearances in Blueberry Park, where she tries to convince people to live their lives opera-free. She feels that operas take up too much time. Also, she has an idea that people who like opera will become unrealistic, and not take their everyday lives seriously. Most of all, she believes that operas are habit-forming, and once a person starts listening to them, it's hard to stop, and one tends to listen to more and more operas until one's life is ruined.

Aunt Terwilliger has pamphlets printed up that she hands out. Her most popular one is called "Grand Opera, an Invention of the Devil."

I got the impression that Aunt Terwilliger made this same speech—the one about how terrible opera was for people, especially the working classes—every morning. The family listened to her politely and sipped their Bull-frog Root Beer.

Aunt Terwilliger was also against eating meat, which is why the Terwilliger-Matthews family never serves any.

When Aunt Terwilliger had finished about opera, Uncle Flipping Hades told us something about the work he did. He's in charge of Research and Development for Bullfrog Industries.

"Then you're a scientist," I said.

"Not just a scientist," Uncle Flipping said. "I am a mad scientist. Just ask my brother-in-law."

"Yes, that's true," Saunders Harrison Matthews II said. "Nobody down at the plant would deny that Flipping is crazy as a bedbug. Mad scientists—really mad ones—aren't that easy to come by. Plenty of companies haven't got one. We're lucky to have him."

"You are, indeed," Uncle Flipping said. "For years I was sane. All I had to think about was how to get bigger bubbles into the root beer and thereby save the company money—less root beer and more bubbles to each bottle, you know. Now that I'm mad, I can get into really interesting stuff. The firm lets me do research on anything I want. They feel that I might stumble on something really important any time. For example, I'm trying to develop an avocado that will grow in the coldest climates right now."

"My father is interested in avocados," I said.

"Then you're Theobald Galt's boy!" Uncle Flipping shouted. "I know your father well. He's a very talented amateur. He has very advanced ideas about avocados. The field of mad science lost a valuable mind when your father went into the synthetic-sausage business."

I had no idea that my father's liking for avocados went beyond the interest of an ordinary consumer. I didn't know whether to be proud of him or worried. Obviously, Rat's family was made up of people who were more or less insane. Uncle Flipping was even proud of it, and so was Rat's father.

Rat's mother, Minna Terwilliger Matthews, hadn't said anything so far to indicate that she was crazy, but I felt fairly certain that she would give us a sign before long. I liked Rat's family. The only crazy people I had met before this were on the order of Miss Sweet. This gang of loonies seemed to have a lot of fun. Besides, I loved my breakfast. Something about Uncle Flipping's high-protein drink was making me feel healthy and wide awake.

"I've got a picture of your father and the prize avocado of 1962," Uncle Flipping said. "I'll run upstairs and get it."

He never came down again.

XV

Uncle Flipping was gone from the table for a long time. While we waited for him to come back with a picture of my father and the prize avocado of 1962, Minna Terwilliger Matthews, Rat's mother, revealed just how crazy she was. I knew she wouldn't disappoint us.

"You know, I suppose," Rat's mother said, "that realtors are all actually beings from other planets. You see, they have to have some sort of disguise or cover so they can move among us Earthlings without drawing attention to themselves. What happened is that in the early 1950s they all came here in flying saucers. One by one, they replaced legitimate real estate brokers. Now all realtors are extraterrestrials."

I was deeply satisfied. Somehow I knew that when she got started, Minna Terwilliger Matthews would turn out to be perhaps the very best of the lot.

"Don't just take my word for it," she was saying. "You can find out for yourselves. They reveal themselves in little ways. Try telling one of them a joke. You'll see that they aren't like us."

Heinz, the non-Chinese Chinese butler, had gone upstairs to see what was keeping Uncle Flipping. When he came back down, he had a serious expression. "Mister Flipping is gone," he said.

Everybody looked solemn.

I was getting upset. He'd just been talking with us, so alive and enthusiastic. "Gone? Dead?" I said, involuntarily.

"No, no," Minna Terwilliger Matthews said, "not dead. Gone."

"Gone?"

"Mister Flipping has a tendency to vanish," Heinz said.

"How do you mean, vanish?" Winston Bongo asked. Of course, it was none of our business what happened in someone else's family, but we liked these loonies, and we were interested.

"Uncle Flipping vanishes fairly often," Rat said, "He disappears in a variety of ways. For example, once we heard a muffled shriek in the night, and he was gone. Another time, there were heavy footsteps in the library, after which he vanished."

"Yes," Saunders Harrison Matthews II added, "and there was the time he vanished, and we found an envelope containing five grapefruit pips under his pillow."

"My favorite was the time we found a stuffed monkey in his place," Aunt Terwilliger said.

"Very often there are ransom notes," Minna Terwilliger Matthews said.

"And, of course," Heinz said, "sometimes he's just gone. This is one of those times. One moment he's here, and then he's not. Gone."

"Let me get this straight," I said. "Uncle Flipping does this all the time?"

"Yes, that's right."

"He's here one moment, and gone the next?"

"Yes."

"And there are shrieks, heavy footsteps, sinister signs, and ransom notes?"

"Exactly."

"But he always comes back?"

"No, that's not quite right," Rat's father said. "He does come back sometimes, but generally we have to get him back."

"There have been times he came back by himself," Heinz said, "and there have been times the police called to say they had him, and would we come and get him. But usually we have to look for him."

"I'm having some trouble following all this," Winston Bongo said. "Is he being kidnapped, or just wandering off?"

"Kidnapped."

"Wanders off."

"A little of each."

It seemed that the family had differences about whether Uncle Flipping Hades' disappearances were voluntary or not.

"Well, what does he say about these disappearances after he gets back?" I asked.

He says different things," Minna Terwilliger Matthews said.

"He says he was kidnapped," Aunt Terwilliger said.

"He says he just went away to be by himself," Saunders Harrison Matthews II said.

"We all look for him," Rat said.

"Miss Rat has found him eight times, all by herself,"

Heinz said, smiling. "She's found him more times than anyone else."

"Except you, Heinz," Rat said. "You've found him more times than I have."

"Yes, but many of those times I had been called by the police to come and collect him," Heinz said. "Those times hardly count."

"I believe all this has some connection with the underworld," Saunders Harrison Matthews II said.

"Oh, Saunders Harrison, not the underworld!" Minna Terwilliger Matthews said.

"Yes, dear, the underworld. I'm sure of it."

"Well, I can't imagine what my brother would have to do with gangsters," Minna Terwilliger Matthews said.

"Not gangsters, dear, the underworld," Saunders Harrison Matthews II said.

"In any case," said Heinz, "shall we go about searching for Mister Flipping in the usual way?"

"Yes, Heinz," Rat's father said. "We'll all keep a sharp lookout for Flipping, especially at night."

"My uncle has never been found, or even turned up, except at night," Rat said to us. "We all more or less go about our business, but we also keep looking for him. There's no telling where he'll turn up. Of course, Heinz and I put a little special effort into looking for him—that's why we've found him more than anyone else."

"You and Heinz are perfect wizards at finding Uncle Flipping, dear," Minna Terwilliger Matthews said.

"Could we help you look for him?" I asked.

"Oh, no, no, there's no need for that," Aunt Terwilliger said, "but thanks all the same. It's a very kind offer."

"But we'd really like to help," Winston Bongo said. "It's our spring vacation, so we don't have anything to do. Besides, we've never looked for anyone missing before."

"Yes," I said, "we'd really like to help."

"Well, that's awfully nice of you both," Saunders Harrison Matthews II said. "Perhaps you'd like to help our little Rat look for her uncle. I could call your parents and let them know that you'll be spending a lot of time over here after dark. I know that Flipping's friend Theobald Galt will agree. He's looked for him once or twice himself. Presumably he can assure Mr. Bongo's parents that looking for Flipping is a wholesome and educational activity."

My father had searched for Flipping Hades Terwilliger? I was learning quite a lot about him this morning. He appeared to have a much more interesting life than I had thought.

"OK," Rat said. "Meet me in front of the Snark at midnight."

"The Snark? I thought we were going to look for your uncle?"

"We are," Rat said. "He's never missed a show. Even when he's missing, he gets in there somehow—in disguise, or crawling out of the sewers. I don't know how."

"He gets the kidnappers to take him there," Rat's mother said. "They're realtors, you know."

"If you know he's going to be at the Snark, it shouldn't be any trouble to find him there," I said.

"It's not that easy," Rat said. "I've only found him at the Snark once. It isn't easy to find disguised people in a dark movie house."

"The forces of the underworld change his outward ap-

pearance," Bentley Saunders Harrison Matthews' father
said.

"I suggest you young people go home and get some rest.
You'll have a long night of searching," Heinz said.

We said good-bye to Saunders Harrison Matthews II,
Aunt Terwilliger, Minna Terwilliger Matthews, and
Heinz, the Chinese butler who wasn't Chinese. Then we
promised Rat that we'd all meet in front of the Snark at
midnight and left for home.

XVI

Winston Bongo and I talked it
over on the bus. Rat's Uncle Flipping was missing, and
that was a usual occurrence. It seemed to both of us that
Uncle Flipping, who was undoubtedly crazy like the rest
of the family, just took it into his head to disappear from
time to time. Winston thought that he'd probably turn up
all by himself if nobody did anything about it. Still, the
idea of a hunt for the missing loony sounded like fun. We
would do our best to help.

I thought it would be a good idea if we took naps. We'd
been up all night and would probably be up all night again,
looking for Flipping. The only thing that still had to be
settled was whether our parents would go along with the

idea of our taking part in the search. I wondered if we should have said something to stop Rat's father, Saunders Harrison Matthews II, from making a call to my father to get permission. After all, it would have been just as easy to sneak out the way we always did.

When I got home, I found out right away that it was going to be all right. "Your old man called from the office," my mother said. "He says that you're going to go out looking for Flipping Hades Terwilliger, and that you'll be out till all hours. He says that it's great fun and that I should let you get some sleep during the day. He also asked me to call the mother of that friend of yours, Winston Bongo, and get her to let Winston go along with this nonsense."

"Did you call her?" I asked.

"Sure," my mother said. "Why not? If my son is going to get sick, lose his hair, and go insane from keeping irregular hours, why shouldn't his best friend?"

"Do you really think people lose their hair and go insane from staying up late?" I asked.

"You can look it up in any medical journal, pal," my mother said. "But if you want to be a baldheaded half-wit by the time you're twenty, that's your business. Just stay away from the Commonists. They're out in force after midnight, just looking for a softheaded kid such as yourself to indoctrinate."

I told my mother I would stay clear of any Commonists I might meet.

"Good boy," she said. "I don't much care if you grow up stupid, or even skinheaded, just so long as you are a decent American and make me proud of you."

My mother always equates stupid people and crazy people. There was no point in getting into an argument about this. If she sensed I was winning, she'd turn crafty and deny everything she'd said. As for me, I was aware that it is possible to be crazy as a coot and still be very bright. Just look at Rat's whole family.

I went off to get some sleep.

I slept until about six in the evening, right through lunch and the whole afternoon. What woke me up was the sound of my father tuning in the evening news on television.

I went into the family room where he was watching.

"I hear you're out to look for Flipping H. Terwilliger," he said. "That's great sport. I've been out looking for him myself."

"What's it like?" I asked.

"That would be telling," my father said. "Just have a good time, and remember that you're apt to find many things besides old Flipping. Here's some operating capital." He gave me five dollars.

"Did you go looking for him recently?" I asked.

"Everybody is entitled to have his own experience," my father said.

I couldn't get another word about the subject out of my father. He just settled down and watched the news. He's like that. He doesn't think it's a good idea to tell his kid too much about experiences and that sort of thing. Still, I wished he would have told me more about the time he went out looking for Uncle Flipping. It seemed I was always finding out interesting things about my father, but he never wanted to talk about them.

"I've got a surprise for you, champ," my mother said.

The surprise was tonight's recipe. It was called Tomato Surprise—tomatoes filled with tuna salad. I wasn't all that surprised. Someday my mother is going to receive an award for using more tuna fish (from American waters) than anyone in history.

I managed to get my supper down, and then, since I was sort of bored and didn't have anything else to do, I went over to Winston Bongo's house.

Winston was sort of restless, too. His parents had agreed that he could participate in the Uncle Flipping hunt. He had had his supper, which, coincidentally, was tuna fish, too. We had the whole evening to kill before meeting Rat in front of the Snark Theater.

"Look," I said, "why don't we go down there early and see the movies?"

"Not a bad idea," Winston said. "We have to be there at midnight anyway."

It was drizzling. We caught the Snark Street bus and headed downtown.

It felt strange to be taking that ride so early in the evening. The bus was fairly full of normal daytime people.

The double bill at the Snark was pretty entertaining. They had *Gidget Goes Hawaiian* and *Gaslight*. Strangely, the theater wasn't nearly as full as it usually is after midnight. We kept an eye out for Uncle Flipping, just in case, but we didn't see him.

When the movies were over, it was still short of midnight by a little more than a half-hour. We looked around for Rat, in case she had gotten there early. She wasn't in sight, so we decided to go across the street to the Hasty

Tasty Café for a snack. We had noticed the Hasty Tasty Café before, but it was always closed. They must shut down at midnight. From the windows of the Hasty Tasty we would be able to keep an eye on the front of the Snark. We'd see Rat if she showed up, or Uncle Flipping, if he arrived before Rat did.

We each got a chocolate-covered doughnut and a glass of milk. The doughnuts tasted like rubber, and the milk was warm. We got our doughnuts and milk at the counter and carried them over to a table near the window. The place was nearly empty. They were getting ready to close. A guy was mopping the floor, and there was a strong smell of ammonia.

Of the few customers in the Hasty Tasty, an abnormal percentage appeared to be weird or crazy. For example, there was a guy who looked like Sherlock Holmes as played in the movies by Basil Rathbone. He had that same big, bent nose, only this guy had his whole face covered with some kind of white make-up, and his hair was painted on—maybe with shoe polish. He had the same sideburns as Basil, but they were paint. The Sherlock Holmes with the painted-on hair was sitting with a short guy in a beat-up tweed jacket, who had a wig made out of a dust mop.

Neither of us was able to finish his rubber doughnut.

We saw Rat across the street. She saw us at the same time and waved to us. We crossed the street and met her under the marquee of the Snark.

XVII

"You guys been here long?" Rat asked.

We told Rat that we'd been there since before eight.

"Any sign of Uncle Flipping?"

"Well, we didn't see him in the theater," Winston Bongo said, "and we kept a pretty careful watch on the Snark from across the street."

"Yes," I said, "except when we were distracted, looking at the guy who looks like Sherlock Holmes, with the painted-on hair."

"A guy who looks like Sherlock Holmes with painted-on hair!" Rat shouted. "Was there a fellow with him with a wig that looks like a mop?"

"Yes, there was. . . ."

"Incredible!" Rat shouted. I'd never seen her so excited.

"Oh, this is serious," Rat said. "This is very serious. This is more serious than anything that's ever happened before. Every time Uncle Flipping disappears or wanders off or goes cuckoo, we worry that it may have something to do with those two, and now you've seen them. Are they still in the café?"

"They were when we left," I said, "just a couple of minutes ago. . . . But who. . ."

"In a minute," Rat said, and sprinted across the street toward the Hasty Tasty. As she ran, we could see that there were no customers at any of the tables. Rat shook the locked door. The lights in the Hasty Tasty Café went out. Apparently there was a back exit, because none of the workers in the café came out, even though we stood around for quite a while.

Rat crossed the street, dejected. "They're probably a block away by now," she said.

"Who are those guys?" we asked.

"Sit down here, and I'll tell you about them."

We sat down on the curb a little way down from the Snark Theater, and Rat told us about the odd-looking men Winston Bongo and I had seen in the Hasty Tasty.

"Years ago my Uncle Flipping took a trip to Iceland," Rat said. "I believe he mentioned to you this morning that he has been trying to cultivate a strain of avocado that will grow in cold climates. This project has been one of the great enthusiasms of his life. When he went to Iceland, he made a sort of safari into the interior. He had lots of scientific equipment with him, things for testing the volcanic soil, instruments to record temperature and humidity, all sorts of timekeeping devices, meteorological devices, cameras, tape recorders—in fact, everything any scientific expedition takes anywhere.

"His intention was to find out exactly what the growing conditions in Iceland were. Having done that, he wanted to duplicate those conditions, artificially, in Bullfrog Industries Laboratories and develop an avocado that could thrive under those conditions. Then, he planned to go back to Iceland and start an experimental avocado plantation.

"When Uncle Flipping came back from Iceland, his behavior was very strange. He stayed in his room for about a month. He wouldn't talk to anybody. He would only eat mandarin orange slices in cans—and the cans had to be opened in his presence. He kept hundreds of tennis balls around him at all times, in plastic lawn-and-leaf bags. Worst of all, Uncle Flipping developed an unreasonable fear of moths. The mere sight of a moth was enough to send him into screaming fits. After a while, the family began to wonder if maybe something had gone wrong with him mentally. My father sent for a famous specialist, Dr. Pierre Ramakrishna, who confirmed our worst fears. Uncle Flipping was suffering from brain fever.

"Dr. Ramakrishna took Uncle Flipping to his sanatorium in Switzerland, where he cured him with his special diet of deep-fried foods. It took months of eating nothing but onion rings, french-fried potatoes, shrimp tempura, hush puppies, and Dr. Ramakrishna's special hot dogs in batter, but Uncle Flipping finally got well and came home.

"It was a long time before Uncle Flipping could talk about his experiences in Iceland. I, personally, still don't know all that happened, but my father does. I do know that after coming back from Dr. Ramakrishna's sanatorium, someone sent my Uncle Flipping a stuffed Indian fruit bat on his birthday every year. When the stuffed fruit bat would arrive, Uncle Flipping would go into his room with a lot of tennis balls.

"Uncle Flipping told my father that an international master criminal was after him. Apparently, he had discovered something, or brought something back from that trip to Iceland that was very valuable. This international criminal of the most dangerous kind knew he had this thing, or had discovered this thing, whatever it is, and Uncle Flipping has lived in mortal fear of him ever since. The brain fever was brought on by my uncle's escape from him. The stuffed fruit bat every year was a signal—one that only Uncle Flipping would understand—that he was still after him."

"And that master criminal was one of the guys we saw in the Hasty Tasty, right?" Winston Bongo asked.

"Wrong," Rat said. "The master criminal is Wallace Nussbaum, the king of crime. The two men you saw were Osgood Sigerson, the greatest living detective, and his friend and companion Dr. Ormond Sacker. The reason they're important is that there can only be one reason for Osgood Sigerson to be in Baconburg, and that is that there is a really important criminal around here. Sigerson's archenemy is a monster by the name of . . . guess."

"Wallace Nussbaum," I guessed.

"That's it," Rat said. "If Sigerson and Sacker are here, it can only be that they're on the trail of Nussbaum, and Nussbaum is on the trail of . . ."

"Uncle Flipping!" I shouted.

"Who's missing and could already be in Nussbaum's clutches," Rat went on. "This is especially serious. Nussbaum is capable of unthinkable acts of cruelty. Not only is he a terrible person, he is the most capable criminal ever to live. He was a major in some South American army, but he was kicked out for terrifying chickens. He holds the world's boomerang record, and he may be the most advanced mathematician alive today. Wallace Nussbaum is no ordinary criminal."

"What would Nussbaum do to Uncle Flipping if he caught him?" Winston asked.

"All I know is that he would stop at nothing," Rat said. "My father told me that once he wanted to get information out of someone, and he kept him in a huge vat of egg foo yung for days until he talked."

"That's horrible," Winston Bongo said.

"This sounds much worse than I had thought," I said. "Don't you think we ought to tell the police?"

"The Terwilliger-Matthews family takes care of its own problems," Rat said. "Besides, Nussbaum has eluded the police all over the world for years. Even Osgood Sigerson hasn't been able to catch him. But you're right—it is worse then we thought, and dangerous. If you fellows want to drop out now, I'll understand."

"What are you going to do?" we asked.

"I'm going to look for my uncle," Rat said.

"Then we're going with you."

"Thanks," Rat said. "You're both good guys."

"Now, hadn't we better get started looking for him?" I asked.

"Yes, indeed," Rat said, "and we'll have to work fast if we want to find him before Nussbaum does. Fortunately, we have the advantage of knowing the city better than he does—at least I do. What's more, I know all the places Uncle Flipping tends to go when he's off on his own. Have either of you ever been to Lower North Aufzoo Street?"

Neither of us had.

"Well, we're going there right away," Rat said.

XVIII

Neither Winston nor I had ever heard of Lower North Aufzoo Street. However, when we got to Upper North Aufzoo Street, we recognized it immediately. It's that curving street that runs along the Baconburg River on the edge of the business district. It's sort of a thoroughfare; there aren't any stores or entrances to buildings along it. There's a sidewalk on either side, a sort of guardrail made of concrete on the river side, and that's all. The cars go whizzing along at about forty-five miles per hour.

What we'd never noticed before about Upper North Aufzoo Street was that there was a concrete staircase leading down from the sidewalk at one point. It looked as though it might be going down to a subway, but it wasn't.

We went down the staircase.

It was quite a contrast. Upper North Aufzoo Street, above us, was nearly deserted and quiet. Lower North Aufzoo Street was a jumble of activity. There were bright yellow fluorescent lights making the street-below-a-street as brilliant as day. Big trucks rumbled along. Some were parked, being loaded or unloaded. Truck drivers and guys who work loading and unloading stood around, chewing on cigars, talking, and joking. There were piles of garbage, broken cartons, and big barrels of wastepaper filling the sidewalk every so often. There was a lot of noise down there. Trucks grinding gears and honking horns and banging into the curb, guys hollering, things bumping and crashing, all amplified by an echo. It was almost too much to take in all at once.

"Welcome to the underworld," Rat said.

A blind guy with a big German shepherd dog was playing his saxophone. The guys from the trucks tossed coins into his cup. There was also a guy doing elaborate pictures on the sidewalk with colored chalk. Rat said he was a screever, the only one in Baconburg. The pictures were pretty good. Most of them were portraits of famous people—the President, TV actors, that sort of thing. There was also a portrait of James Dean. This got Rat started, talking about how the great tragedy of her life was that James Dean had died before she was born. She said she wanted to hitchhike to Hollywood someday and visit his grave.

"What is this place?" I asked.

"It's fairly obvious," Rat said. "This is the city beneath the city. There is where the guts are. It goes round the clock. I'm sort of surprised you didn't know it was here. You see, all the truck deliveries to the business district come through here. Also, this is where all the garbage gets picked up. Besides that, this is how you get into the network of steam pipes that heat all the big office buildings. Some of the guys you see coming and going are maintenance workers. Some work in the sewers or installing the underground phone lines; others just get to and from work through here—janitors, clean-up people, night watchmen, all of those. You can get in a service elevator here and go up into the big hotels and office buildings and stores. And then there are people who live by trading with the people who come through here, or beg from them, or rip them off. There's even music and art down here—the saxophone player and the screever. And there's food and drink. In fact, let's stop into Bignose's Cafeteria. There's a chance Uncle Flipping will be in there at this hour."

There were a few bars lining Lower North Aufzoo Street. Most of them had red neon signs that said 50¢ A DRINK. There was also a fairly large cafeteria, brightly lit inside, with big plate-glass windows. A sign made of blue neon tubing over the windows said BIGNOSE'S CAFE-TERIA. A big red neon sign that flashed on and off said EAT-EAT-EAT.

We went in.

"That's Bignose," Rat said.

We could have guessed. Bignose was about five foot nothing, with a truly enormous honker. He was little and skinny and insignificant except for his beak. He was like a nose with a man attached.

"Come over here, boys," Bignose said from behind the steam table. He had such a deep voice that it made the windows vibrate when he spoke and drowned out all the noise coming from outside. "I've got spaghetti and fried squid tonight."

"We'll just have a snack, Bignose," Rat said. "Has my uncle been in?"

"Three coffees and three Napoleons," Bignose said, fill-ing three big mugs, which he held in one hand. "I think maybe I saw him; maybe it was last night. It was pretty busy awhile ago. I get confused. Here, gimmie. I'll punch your tickets."

Bignose pushed three Napoleons and three cups of coffee across the high glass counter at us and held out his hand. Rat had taken three tickets from a little machine near the door as we came in. She gave them to Bignose, who punched them with a conductor's punch and handed them back.

Rat gave us each a punched ticket and a Napoleon and a cup.

The way it works at Bignose's is this: You get your ticket punched with the amount of whatever you pick up at the counter. Then, when you're leaving, you present your ticket at the cash register, and that's how much you pay. I'd never seen that system before. I also had never seen a Napoleon before. It's a pastry. It's flaky and creamy, and it tastes great! The coffee had a lot of milk in it. It was pretty good, too.

I had two Napoleons, Winston had two, Rat had three.

While we were sitting in Bignose's, a green wagon done up like a sort of house, and drawn by a big white horse, rattled by.

"What's that?" I asked

"Gypsies," Rat said. "Gypsies hang out down here. See over there?"

If we leaned over, and looked out the window down Lower North Aufzoo Street, we could see a woman in a long skirt, chopping wood outside another one of those green house-type wagons. There was a stovepipe sticking out the top. It was smoking.

We took our tickets to the cash register and paid for our

coffees and Napoleons. The lady at the cash register was smoking a cigarette. She had carrot red hair, and a lot of lipstick.

We went outside into the noise and bustle of the street.

"What now?" Winston Bongo asked.

"Now we take a walk," Rat said. "That way."

Rat indicated the end of Lower North Aufzoo Street, past the gypsy wagons, where the bright yellow lights stopped and the street curved away into darkness. We started walking. Away from the noise and brightness, it smelled musty. Now and then we got a whiff of wood-smoke from the gypsies' stoves. Soon, the gypsies were behind us. The street seemed to be getting smaller. It was like walking into a tunnel.

XIX

I can't say I liked the part of Lower North Aufzoo Street we were now walking along as much as the area around Bignose's Cafeteria. It was damp and sour-smelling. Instead of the bright fluorescent lights, old-fashioned, dim, yellow-white streetlamps were fastened to the concrete wall every so often. Each lamp made a puddle of light around it. In between it was pretty dark.

Now and then a truck would rumble by, making a lot of noise. The ceiling was much lower than in the bright part of Lower North Aufzoo Street, and the rush of air and the roar of the engines as the trucks went by made us uncomfortable. It was even more uncomfortable after they passed, because it seemed much darker after the brightness of the headlights.

"This is a great place to get mugged," Winston Bongo said.

"I'll say," I said.

There were fragments of trash on the sidewalk, and every now and then I would feel something squishy beneath my feet.

"I'll bet there are rats down here," I said.

"My fellow rats," Rat said.

A lot of the time, we walked without saying anything. I was looking everywhere for rats and muggers in the shadows. We seemed to be going downhill.

I really didn't like it down there. I was reminded of a depressing Polish movie I had seen at the Snark once. It was all about people getting lost in the sewers underneath Warsaw in World War II. The air got fouler the farther we went. I wanted to turn around and go back. I wanted to go back to Bignose's. If Winston had said anything about going back, I would have agreed with him. I'm sure that if I had suggested going back, he would have agreed with me. He was humming tunelessly to himself, which he only does when he is very displeased with what is happening. But Winston didn't say anything, and neither did I. We just went along with Rat. The steel taps on Rat's shoes made an echo in the dark tunnel street.

Then we saw something! Something dark and rumpled and shapeless was blocking the pavement ahead of us, not far from a streetlamp!

I knew what it was at once, but I didn't want it to be what it was. I tried to think of something else it could be —something besides a human body.

It couldn't have been anything else. We slowed down, almost to a stop.

"Oh, God, suppose it's someone dead?" I said.

"Suppose it isn't," Winston said.

We could make out the figure now. Someone wrapped in something was sitting propped with its back against the wall. Long, skinny legs were stretched across the pavement. I could see skinny ankles and big, pointy shoes.

We had come to a full stop a few paces from the figure —far enough to turn and run like mad if it happened to be someone we should run from.

The figure didn't move. We didn't move.

"I think it is someone dead," I said. "I can't see him breathing."

"Come on, there's three of us," Rat said. "There's nothing to be scared of." Nobody moved.

Then we heard a sound. It was horrible. It was unearthly. It was something between moaning and cooing. A high-pitched sort of metallic voice was saying, "*Aaook, aaaaoook, oooook, koooo!*"

"Oh, no!" Winston said.

"What is that?" Rat said.

"Let's go," I said.

"*Ooook, oooook, puk-puk-puk*," said the voice.

"That's a chicken!" Rat said.

The figure slumped against the wall stirred. The old black man rearranged the raincoat that was wrapped around him. When he shifted position, we could see the chicken in his upturned hat on the pavement beside him.

"It's that guy! The one with the performing chicken!" Winston said. "You see him everywhere!"

"Oh! People!" the old man said, getting to his feet. "This is upsetting. This is rather embarrassing. I was just resting —that is, the chicken and I. I'm quite nonplussed. I really don't know what to say. You see, I wouldn't want it known that I make a practice of taking naps on the pavement on Lower North Aufzoo Street. Really, I was just feeling tired, and so I sat down. I'm not a vagabond. I have a home to go to. Please promise me you won't mention this to anyone."

We promised we wouldn't.

"Thank you, young people," the old man said. "Adverse publicity can be a real nuisance. As an impresario, I just can't afford to be thought of as a person who takes naps in the street. Not that I mind for myself, but it might damage the chances of my protégé." He gestured toward the chicken. "This is Dharmawati, the greatest performing chicken of the age."

The chicken bowed.

We bowed to the chicken.

"And I am Captain Shep Nesterman," the old guy said. "May I know whom I have the pleasure of addressing?"

We introduced ourselves.

"I am delighted to make your acquaintance," Captain Shep Nesterman said. Dharmawati, the performing chicken, hopped onto his shoulder and then onto his head, and he placed his hat over her. "Are you walking?" the chicken trainer asked. "I would be pleased to accompany you."

"We were going that way," Rat said.

"Perfect!" said Captain Shep Nesterman. "I was planning to go that way myself. Now I'll have the pleasure of your company, if it would not be an imposition."

"Not at all," Winston said.

"No, no, it would be our pleasure," I said.

"We'd be delighted if you'd come along with us," Rat said.

Something about the way Captain Shep Nesterman talked made all of us behave in a super-polite manner.

We began to walk. Captain Shep Nesterman made polite conversation with us, and Dharmawati, the greatest performing chicken of the age, occasionally clucked under his hat.

The walk through the dark part of Lower North Aufzoo Street was much more pleasant now that Captain Shep Nesterman had joined us. There wasn't any reason to feel more secure—an old man like that wasn't likely to be any help if we were set upon by muggers—but somehow he gave us confidence. It was as if he belonged down there, or at least knew the place well enough to be unafraid to go to sleep there.

At one point we came to a puddle that stretched from one wall of the tunnel street to the other. It was too wide to jump over, so we had no choice but to walk through it. We got soaked to the ankles.

After the puddle, the street seemed to incline slightly upward. No doubt that had been the lowest point, and that was why the water had collected there.

Soon, the sour, damp, underground smell began to be mixed with whiffs of fresh air and the smell of rusty iron. The ceiling was getting higher.

Then the concrete walls gave way to a network of big

iron girders. Fresh air poured through. We could see the night sky, which seemed bright after the darkness of the tunnel. Actually, it was bright, lit up with the glow of the lights of Baconburg. But there weren't any lights near us. On the other side of the iron girders, there seemed to be just open space and the smell of earth and things growing.

The ceiling was high above us now, and I realized that we were walking under a sort of causeway. Above us was Upper North Aufzoo Street. Now and then, we could hear a car or truck rumble along the elevated roadway.

Then Upper North Aufzoo Street veered away to the right, and we were out under the sky. The old-fashioned streetlamps were farther apart now and mounted on iron lampposts. There were some beaten-up iron fences bordering the sidewalk, and behind them what seemed to be fields.

"We're out in the sticks!" Winston said.

XX

"Haven't you ever been in Tintown before?" Rat asked.

Winston and I had never heard of Tintown, much less been there.

"Tintown gets its name," Captain Shep Nesterman said,

"from the improvised houses here. There used to be a lot of them. During hard times in the past, people sort of camped out here. They made shacks and shanties out of old packing crates, cardboard, and abandoned cars. Flattened tin cans were a popular roofing material—hence the name. The land belonged to the city of Baconburg. There was a plan to make a railroad yard here, but it never got built. Times got better, and the squatters—the people who had built the houses—went away, most of them. But some of them stayed. If you squat on land—build a house on it —and no one claims the land for a certain period of time, the land becomes yours, after a fashion. At least, no one can make you move off."

"My father told me that there used to be hundreds of slapped-together houses along this street, Scrap Ankle Road," Rat said.

"Yes, it was quite a place," Captain Shep Nesterman said. "It was like a little city unto itself. I was once mayor of Tintown."

"You were?"

"Oh, yes. We had a mayor, a police department, schools, places of entertainment. It was really a wonderful place. The city of Baconburg didn't provide any services because it regarded the whole settlement as illegal, so we made our own government. Of course, all that is gone now. Now there are just a handful of houses, and Beanbender's Beer Garden."

"Beanbender's Beer Garden?"

"Oh, a wonderful place! It's still going strong. Beanbender's was always *the* place to go in Tintown. You can just see the lights of Beanbender's now."

94

In the distance, way down Scrap Ankle Road, we could see some dim, flickering lights. They had a warmer color than electric lights, and as we got closer we could see that they were from kerosene lanterns. It turned out that there wasn't much, if any, electricity in Tintown.

Turning around, we could see the tall buildings of Baconburg, mostly dark against the night sky. Our walk underground, down Lower North Aufzoo Street, had taken us in a big, curving sweep below the business district, away from the river, and out into this place, which seemed to be on lower ground than the rest of the city. It was a big, flat, open plain that was swampy in spots, with clumps of tall swamp grasses and plants here and there. The flat place must have gone on for at least a couple of miles in all directions.

Beanbender's was a strange-looking structure. At first, it was hard to get any idea of its shape; it just seemed to be a collection of odd-looking dark lumps in the night. Then we could see that Beanbender's was made up of a number of dead trucks and a couple of railroad cars arranged in a circle, like covered wagons in the movies, made into a circle for protection against the Indians.

All the dead trucks and railroad cars were covered with wooden shingles and banked with earth and gravel above the wheels. A number of kerosene lanterns were fastened to the outside of the circle. There was a door, with a lantern on either side, lighting up a sign painted on a board. BEANBENDER'S, it said.

When we walked into Beanbender's we were smacked in the face by a whole lot of warmth, light, and good smells. There were lots of people in the open areas made by the trucks and railroad cars. They were sitting at tables made of old giant cable spools and old doors laid across sawhorses. The whole place was lighted by candles stuck in bottles and kerosene lamps, and together with the wood shingles that were tacked onto the trucks and railroad cars, the dozens of flames made a warm, reddish glow under the dark sky.

In the middle of the circle was a big iron thing—sort of a basket—and some logs were burning in it, making more friendly light, good smells, and crackling noises.

There was a guy playing a little accordion, and some people were singing along with him. People had big mugs of beer and big, crisp-looking sausages and baked potatoes in their hands. They held the sausages and the baked potatoes wrapped in a paper napkin and took bites of them between swigs of beer. Even though it was late at night, three or four little kids ran around among the tables.

It was the greatest place I had ever seen.

Winston Bongo thought so, too. Rat, of course, had been there before. "Have a beer?" she asked.

I had tasted beer before, and I hadn't liked it. It was sour and sort of soapy tasting. I never understood why anybody wanted to drink it. However, in Beanbender's it seemed that holding a mug of beer in one's hand was the thing to do, so I went up to the bar and got one along with Rat and Winston and Captain Shep Nesterman.

Beanbender's beer was nothing like the stuff in cans that my father drinks. It had a nutty taste, and it was cold and good. The guy at the bar was Ben Beanbender, the owner of the beer garden. He didn't ask us for identification or anything. He just filled mugs from a big barrel and handed them to us. I also got a baked potato. Ben Beanbender poked a hole in one end with his thumb, slapped in a hunk of butter, salted and peppered the potato, wrapped it in a napkin, and handed it to me. It was great! The potato was almost too hot to hold, and the salty butter dribbled onto my sleeve. It tasted just fantastic with the beer. The beer and the baked potato cost fifty cents. It's the best deal in Baconburg.

"Let's find a place to sit," Captain Shep Nesterman said, "and enjoy the passing parade."

I didn't understand exactly what Captain Nesterman meant at first, about enjoying the passing parade. I was too wrapped up with my first impressions of Beanbender's and the fabulous taste of my beer and baked potato to really take in what turned out to be the best thing about Ben Beanbender's Beer Garden in Tintown.

It's the greatest place to watch people in this world!

For sheer variety of types of human beings, bizarre characters, ugly men, beautiful women, odd costumes, shapes and sizes, and strange styles of speaking, singing, moving, and dancing, there simply can't possibly be any place better.

What's more, everybody talks to everybody else in Beanbender's. Just sitting there, you get involved in conversations, arguments, and philosophical disputes. People just sit down at your table and start talking.

XXI

Captain Shep Nesterman had turned his hat upside down on the table, and Dharmawati, the performing chicken, had settled down in it. Now and then, Captain Shep Nesterman would give Dharmawati a sip of his beer or a nibble of his baked potato. Apparently, Captain Shep Nesterman was well known at Beanbender's, because a lot of people said hello to him and asked if he and Dharmawati were going to perform that evening.

"We may perform later," Captain Shep Nesterman would say, "if our guitarist shows up."

A few faces in the crowd were familiar. I thought I recognized some of the people from Blueberry Park. I definitely recognized the devil's-gonna-get-you man. He was sitting quietly with two pretty girls, sipping his beer.

A fellow in a turban, with a bushy, black beard, sat down.

"Shim bwa la boo," the guy in the turban said.

"Bwa loo sha bim," Captain Shep Nesterman said.

"May your eyebrows be blessed, brother," said the guy in the turban.

"May angels sit upon your ear," said Captain Shep Nesterman.

"How do you think St. Louis will do in the National League next season?" the guy in the turban asked.

"Not as well as Pittsburgh, unless Mac Schwartz's shoulder gets better," Captain Shep Nesterman said.

"Yeah, he was having a good season until he got injured," the guy in the turban said.

"Best pitcher in the league," Captain Shep Nesterman said.

"Yeah . . . well, sha la boo shim," said the guy in the turban.

"Sha loo sha loo," said Captain Shep Nesterman.

The guy in the turban got up and left.

"Excuse me for not introducing you," Captain Shep Nesterman said. "He's the Grand Shapoo of the Church of the Holy Home Run, and with the least encouragement he'd sit here talking baseball and religion until we were all bored out of our minds."

The guy with the accordion was dancing on a table with a glass of beer on his head. He squatted down and kicked out with one leg and then the other, playing the little accordion all the time and not spilling a drop of beer. Everybody clapped in rhythm, and he kept it up for about five minutes. At the end of his dance, the accordion player shouted, "Fooey on the Czar!" and poured the glass of beer over his own head. Everybody clapped and threw money. We threw some dimes. The accordion player waved his hand over his head and picked up the money.

Captain Shep Nesterman applauded politely. "An energetic fellow," he said, "but he is very limited in his repertoire. I don't mean to put him down, but I've seen that same table-dancing routine a hundred times. You'll see a really creative performance later, if Paco shows up."

A skinny, nervous fellow sat down. "Hello, hello, hello," he said, shaking hands with each of us. "Captain

Nesterman," the skinny, nervous fellow said, "I have done it! As you know, I started out by painting a picture of my bedroom, with all its contents. That was wrong. It didn't say what I wanted to say. I thought about it, and threw out my bedroom chair. Then I painted a picture of my bedroom without the chair. That was a little better, but it still did not convey my innermost thoughts. So then I threw out my chest of drawers and painted the bedroom without the chair and chest of drawers. By this time, I knew I was on the right track. I threw out my bed, my bedside table, my alarm clock, the picture of the Grand Shapoo of the Church of the Holy Home Run that used to hang on my wall. Then I painted my bedroom with absolutely nothing in it. I really thought I was all the way there, but somehow it didn't quite work. I was miserable. For weeks I lay on the floor, unable to sleep, thinking, thinking, thinking. I tell you, Captain Nesterman, I wasn't sure I would come out of this creative crisis as a sane person. I was at the end of my rope, when it came upon me in a burst of inspiration! All this time, I had been trying to paint my bedroom! Get it? I had been trying to *paint my bedroom*! But I had not had the actual pure experience of painting my bedroom! I was excited, I can tell you! I went out and got paint, white paint, pure white. I painted the walls of my bedroom. I painted the ceiling. I painted the floor. I painted the window, both the frame and the glass. I painted the door and the doorknob. In short, I painted every single part of my bedroom pure white, including the lightbulb in the ceiling. Then I went and got my canvas and brushes, and I painted a picture of my bedroom. It came out perfectly!"

"Has anyone seen the painting?" Captain Shep Nesterman asked.

"Seen it?" the excited, skinny painter shouted. "The Museum of Modern Art in New York has bought it for fifty thousand dollars! Which reminds me, here's the three dollars I owe you. I have to go now—I'm painting my bathroom." The skinny painter shook hands all round again and hurried off.

"I knew he'd be a success," Captain Shep Nesterman said. "What a talented fellow."

A woman with a rag around her head and lots of jingly gold jewelry was the next person to sit down with us. Her name was Madame Zabonga. She offered to tell our fortunes by examing the beer and butter stains on our sleeves. It cost a quarter. I had her tell mine. She looked at the places where the butter from my baked potato had dripped and told me a whole lot of things about myself. She said that I was a nice boy, and that I would grow up to be a nice man, and that I didn't like school, and that I liked to eat and sleep. None of this seemed to be worth a quarter. Then she said that I would share in a secret and experience danger. I was embarrassed to ask for my money back, so I didn't, but I thought the whole experience was a load of horseradish. I was sorry I had wasted my money. I could have bought another beer or a baked potato with that quarter.

Paco arrived. Paco was the guitar player who accompanied Captain Shep Nesterman and Dharmawati, the performing chicken, at least when they performed at Ben Beanbender's Beer Garden in Tintown. Paco had black hair, parted in the middle and slicked down with grease.

He also had a thick black moustache that curled up at the ends.

Paco greeted us gravely and asked Captain Shep Nesterman if he and Dharmawati wished to perform that evening.

"In fact, Dharmawati is in excellent voice, and feeling limber, and so am I," Captain Shep Nesterman said.

Paco, who was always serious, unsnapped his guitar case and took out the instrument. Then he carried a chair to the middle of the room, not far from the fireplace. When the people saw Paco, they all began to clap and shout. They got up and dragged tables and chairs away, so there was an open space in the middle of the beer garden, with Paco sitting to one side of it. Someone brought Paco a little footstool, and he put one foot on it. Then, with the guitar balanced on his raised knee, he spent a long time tuning it, with his head bent down, listening to sounds so soft nobody in the place could hear them.

When Paco was satisfied that the guitar was in tune, he strummed a single loud chord and nodded to Captain Shep Nesterman. Captain Shep Nesterman arose and, carrying Dharmawati on his wrist, wings flapping, he walked into the firelight.

The crowd went wild. There was a lot of applause and cheering.

Captain Shep Nesterman nodded to Paco. Paco nodded to Captain Shep Nesterman. The crowd was silent.

Then Captain Shep Nesterman put Dharmawati on the floor. He stood up very straight, put his arms in a certain position—one in front of him and one in back—and stamped his foot very loudly.

Paco strummed a few chords.

Captain Shep Nesterman stamped his feet a lot of times in rapid succession. He kept his back very straight and did subtle things with his arms. He looked good.

Captain Shep Nesterman was getting into some tricky steps. As his movements got more complicated, Paco's playing got fancier. It was getting pretty good. Captain Nesterman was really stamping around pretty well. Up to this point, Dharmawati had just stood there next to Paco. Then she began to sing! It was a wild sound; a sort of high-pitched moaning and crowing and crooning. It sounded wild, and sort of sad. Paco watched Captain Shep Nesterman, and what he played depended on what Captain Shep Nesterman did in his foot-stamping dance. Sometimes Dharmawati would sing to Captain Shep Nesterman's dancing, and sometimes Captain Shep Nesterman would dance to Dharmawati's singing. Sometimes Paco would sing along with Dharmawati, and sometimes Paco would take a solo. Then Captain Shep Nesterman would wait, and Dharmawati would wait, until he was through. It was really great! Each of them was making up what he or she was doing as they went along, and the whole thing blended together. The audience was really going crazy. They were great performers—all of them—including the chicken.

XXII

Captain Shep Nesterman finished up his act by taking two sets of castanets out of his pocket and adding their clicking to the stamping, strumming, and singing. The last bit of the act—the part with the castanets—was particularly wild and active, and Dharmawati got off some of her best sounds. The crowd went wild when it was over. They would have shouted the roof down if there had been a roof. There was a shower of money. People were throwing coins, and coins wrapped in dollar bills, and fives and tens. Captain Shep Nesterman and Paco shoveled up the money while Dharmawati took the bows.

It really was a great performance. I never thought I would be wildly applauding a singing chicken, but I was. It wasn't just the novelty of a singing chicken either—she was really good! After hearing her sing, I had a lot more respect for Dharmawati than I'd had previously.

We were so wrapped up in the performance of Captain Shep Nesterman and his ensemble that we failed to notice that someone had joined us at our table during the singing, dancing, guitar playing, and castanet clicking. As Captain Shep Nesterman, Paco, and Dharmawati made their way back to our table, we became aware that a very fat man in a white suit was seated with us, his chair pushed back a little way so that he would have been out of our field of vision when we were watching the entertainment.

"Ah! Mr. Gutzman!" Captain Shep Nesterman said as he approached the table.

"I'd like to buy that bird," the fat man said in a voice that seemed to rumble from deep within his suit.

"So you've told me a hundred times at least," Captain Shep Nesterman said, "but Dharmawati and Paco and I are a team. The chicken is not for sale."

"I like you, Captain Nesterman," Mr. Gutzman said. "You're a man who likes a chicken, a rare quality in these evil times."

Captain Shep Nesterman introduced us to Mr. Gutzman. He said that Mr. Gutzman was an old friend of his and only appeared to be a shady character. In reality, he said, Mr. Gutzman was only a sort of part-time crook.

Mr. Gutzman chuckled. "Oh, ho, ho, you're a caution, Captain Nesterman. A real caution. But as much as I enjoy sitting here and exchanging witticisms with you, I must get to business. I bring a message. It is this: A certain party would like to see the three young people in private."

"And that certain party is?" Captain Shep Nesterman asked.

Mr. Gutzman leaned forward. He made a trumpet of his hand and whispered, "The man with the secret information, the same one who sent you to the underground street tonight."

"In that case," Captain Shep Nesterman said, "you three had better go with Mr. Gutzman here and see whoever he's talking about. For my part, I have no idea who or what he means."

"Oh, ho, ho, you're a real pleasure to deal with, Captain," Mr. Gutzman said. "Upon my word, you are. Well, young people, kindly follow me."

Mr. Gutzman got to his feet with considerable effort and made his way through the crowded beer garden. We exchanged looks and followed him.

As we moved away from the table, Paco arrived with three mugs of beer for Captain Shep Nesterman, Dharmawati, and himself.

"We'll be right here, kids!" Captain Shep Nesterman called after us.

Mr. Gutzman led us to a dark corner of Beanbender's Beer Garden. In the side of one of the shingled-over railroad cars, there was a door. Mr. Gutzman knocked four times, and then twice. The door opened. A very large, muscular man was inside. He kept his face turned away from us and stayed in the shadows.

"It's me—Gutzman," Mr. Gutzman said. "Tell a certain party that the three kids are here."

The big, muscular figure disappeared into the dark interior of the railroad car. This was a little scary. I wondered why we were letting this fat, sinister character take us inside a dark railroad car. For all we knew, he was planning to kill us, or hold us for ransom.

Mr. Gutzman must have sensed the thoughts I was having—and the thoughts of Rat and Winston Bongo, too. "I assure you, there is nothing to fear," he said. "A certain party wishes to speak to you, that is all."

"Then why doesn't he just come out here and speak to us?" Winston Bongo asked.

"That is none of my business," Mr. Gutzman said. "I was simply told to bring you to a certain party, just as Captain Nesterman was told to make sure that you turned up at Beanbender's."

That was something that hadn't occurred to me. We hadn't met Captain Shep Nesterman by accident; he had been waiting for us in the underground street!

The heavyweight guy came back to the door. "He says to send them in," he said. "You go and have a beer with Captain Nesterman, Gutzman. You won't be needed again tonight."

We stepped through the door in the side of the railroad car. It was fairly dark inside and hung with heavy curtains, which made a sort of passageway. "Go that way," the big guy said, "and knock on the door at the end." We never saw his face.

I was more or less terrified as we walked along the corridor made of curtains. There was a dim green lightbulb that gave just enough light to see by. The drapes seemed to be a sort of purplish color.

We arrived at the door, which was a big steel one, and knocked.

"Enter!" said a muffled voice on the other side.

We pushed the door open. We entered a room too dimly lit to really see anything in, but it had the feeling of being well furnished. Sitting at a desk, next to a green lamp that hardly gave any light, was a figure wearing a hooded robe. It was like a monk's robe. He had his hood up, and his face was entirely hidden in shadow. I felt like running away.

"Thank you for coming," said the hooded figure. There was something familiar about the muffled voice coming from within the hood. I couldn't place it; I thought maybe he sounded like some movie actor, but I couldn't think which one.

"I regret there are no chairs for you," the hooded person said. "I will try to keep this interview as brief as possible."

It can't be too brief for me, I thought.

XXIII

"Also, please excuse me for not introducing myself," the hood said. "There are reasons why it is best that you should not know my identity. Now, I will ask you to give an account of your activities this evening. Before you begin, I will tell you that I know that you are looking for a certain party—a certain Flipping Hades Terwilliger. Now, tell me what you did from, say, midnight on."

We looked at each other. It was confusing. Who was this guy in the hood? He could easily have been in cahoots with Wallace Nussbaum. In fact, he could have been Wallace Nussbaum himself. I decided I'd better be careful of what I'd say. Winston and Rat had made the same decision.

"We just . . . uh . . . sort of fooled around," Winston said.

"That's right," Rat said, "while looking for my Uncle

Flipping, of course. . . . We fooled around and sort of vaguely looked for my uncle."

"Yes," I said. "You know, we ate some stuff in an all-night cafeteria, and we sort of walked around and told jokes and just sort of . . . uh . . . fooled around."

"And this Uncle Flipping? Why are you looking for him?" the man in the hood asked.

"Well, they're worried about him at home," Rat said. "Our butler, Heinz, isn't feeling well, and they might have to call the doctor, and they're worried that Uncle Flipping doesn't know that . . . uh . . . Heinz isn't feeling well," Rat said.

"And is that why you're looking for Flipping Hades Terwilliger?" the man in the hood asked.

"Yes, well, you see, he didn't say where he was going," Winston Bongo said.

"And he didn't say when he'd be back," I said.

"And you know nothing about a man named Wallace Nussbaum?" the hooded man asked.

"Who?"

"You know nothing of a man named Wallace Nussbaum?"

"Who's that?"

"And have you ever heard of Osgood Sigerson?"

"Osgood who? We've never heard of him. We don't know what you're talking about."

"I think you know very well what I'm talking about. I think you know who Osgood Sigerson is, and I want to know if you've seen him tonight."

"Mister, we came here with Captain Shep Nesterman, had a beer and a baked potato, sat around for a while, and that's all. We don't know anything about any Nussbaum or Sigerson. We don't know what you're talking about."

"What would you say if I told you that something very unpleasant might happen to you unless you told the truth? You know, no one knows you are here, and I can get very nasty if I want to."

"We're telling you the truth," Winston Bongo said. "Besides, it's not a good idea to threaten us. We're plenty strong—Miss Matthews is armed—and I know quite a lot about self-defense. I'm the nephew of the Mighty Gorilla, and he's taught me lots of tricks."

"I'm sure he has, Winston Bongo," said Osgood Sigerson, laughing and throwing back his hood. "As a matter of fact, it was your uncle, the Mighty Gorilla, who was so careful to keep his back turned when you came in. I have hired him as a bodyguard and general man-of-all-work during my present . . . activity. I do apologize to you all for the little dramatic display. It was essential that I find out how well you can keep a secret, even under adverse conditions. I never doubted you, but we're playing a dangerous game, and I had to be sure that you were people I could count on."

Osgood Sigerson was as weird-looking as ever with his painted-on sideburns. While he was talking, he took out a pipe and began smoking some tobacco, which smelled even fouler than the rotten cigarettes that Rat smoked.

"Mr. Sigerson," Rat said, "do you know where my uncle is? Does Nussbaum have him?"

"I'll tell you everything," Osgood Sigerson said, "but first, let's have some lights on. Let me get out of this nasty hot robe, and we'll have a slice of avocado pie. Then we'll have a talk about the events of this night."

XXIV

The heavyweight guy came back. This time we could see his face.

"Hello, nephew," the fireplug said.

"Hello, Uncle Gorilla," Winston Bongo said. He introduced Rat and me to his uncle. We shook hands. It was the first time I had ever met a celebrity.

"Now for the avocado pie!" Osgood Sigerson said. On a side table there was a pie covered with a sheet of plastic wrap, some paper plates, and a knife. "I'm sorry we don't have any utensils," Osgood Sigerson said, "but fingers were made before forks, you know."

It was when Osgood Sigerson mentioned the avocado pie that I first remembered something I hadn't thought of for a couple of hours. What with all the excitement and possibility of danger, the fascinating atmosphere of Beanbender's Beer Garden, and being afraid of the mysterious man in the hood, I had neglected the obvious fact that I was dealing with crazy people here. Now, it has to be understood that I liked Rat very much, and her family, too, but there wasn't any question that they were stark, raving mad. And Captain Shep Nesterman was not your normal type of person either. I mean, who in his right mind dances with a chicken? Of course, Osgood Sigerson, the world's greatest detective according to Rat, with his white clown make-up and painted-on sideburns, had to be regarded as at least extremely eccentric. All this had temporarily escaped me, but when he mentioned the avocado pie, it all came back.

By the way, the pie tasted just as horrible as I thought it would.

"Avocados are also called alligator pears. Did you know that?" Osgood Sigerson asked as he took a second helping. "In answer to the question someone asked a little while ago," Osgood Sigerson said, munching his avocado pie, "the answer is yes."

"Yes?"

"Yes."

"Yes what?" Winston, Rat, and I were thoroughly confused.

"Yes, I believe he has him."

"He? Has who?"

"Didn't someone ask me whether I thought that Mr. Flipping Hades Terwilliger was in the hands of that fiend Wallace Nussbaum?"

"You think Nussbaum has my uncle?" Rat asked.

"I believe it may be so. Right now, my friend and associate Dr. Sacker is out checking on a few details for me. When he comes back and makes his report, based on the information he brings me, I will be able to deduce whether or not Nussbaum holds your uncle captive. I do everything by deduction, you know. You give me an insignificant fact or two, and I can figure out just about anything. Dr. Sacker is first-rate at accumulating insignificant facts. He's a prince of a fellow. Oh, my! I should have saved him a slice of avocado pie, and I've eaten the last one. Mr. Gorilla, would you be kind enough to dash down to the All-Night Zen Bakery to pick up another avocado pie? Also, see if they have any avocado eclairs, avocado-chip cookies, anything at all as long as it has avocado in it. There's a good fellow. You'll have lots of time to chat with your nephew later."

The Mighty Gorilla left. I sank into a chair. Osgood Sigerson licked the tip of his finger and ran it around the inside of the pie plate, picking up avocado crumbs. Rat and Winston looked at one another without expression. I knew what they were thinking. My own father is an avocado addict, and I know how depressing it can be to deal with one.

Sure enough, Osgood Sigerson launched immediately into a long discussion of avocado pastries around the world. I felt right at home, but I could tell that Rat and Winston were suffering intensely.

Rat made an attempt to change the subject. "Mr. Sigerson, you say that you believe Wallace Nussbaum has kidnapped my uncle."

"Yes, yes," Osgood Sigerson said. "As soon as Dr. Sacker returns with the information I asked him to gather, I'll explain everything in detail. Now, where was I? Oh, yes. In Bombay, India, I once was privileged to sample some avocado fritters at the home of Chief Inspector Mookerjee of the Bombay Metropolitan Constabulary. They were deep-fried and folded into a triangular shape. Good? I tell you, they were absolutely marvelous. They were not unlike a banana-and-avocado fritter I enjoyed in Dar es Salaam. . . ."

He went on like that. Sigerson seemed never to run out

of avocado stories. Many of them I recognized from my father's store of information about the disgusting things. Apparently these were stories well known among avocado slaves the world over. I knew all about the banana-and-avocado fritters in Dar es Salaam, and have always hoped and prayed that I would be able to live my life without having to eat one.

It was a big relief when the Mighty Gorilla came back with an armload of avocado pastries. A minute or two later, Dr. Ormond Sacker arrived.

We were introduced to the great detective's friend and associate. Osgood Sigerson handed around cheese-and-avocado Danishes, and we all settled down to listen to Ormond Sacker's report.

XXV

Dr. Ormond Sacker was dressed in a suit made of a fuzzy plaid material. He wore a bowler hat of dark green, under which he wore his wig, which looked like a dust mop. Out of his plaid waistcoat he dug a rumpled sheet of paper, and, holding a cheese-and-avocado Danish in one hand and the sheet of paper in the other, he began to speak.

"I've made some notes, Sigerson, of the matters you requested me to observe. First of all, I went to the Baconburg hay-and-feed dealer, as you requested. There I learned that a number of bales of straw had been sold to a man with blue-tinted eyeglasses and a heavy foreign accent. The dealer did not deliver them. They were picked up in a taxicab by the man who had made the purchase. I then went to the center of town and made enquiries of the proprietor of the out-of-town-newspaper stand. Only one copy of the *Times of Iceland* was sold today—to a man with blue-tinted eyeglasses. The proprietor, a Mr. Fat Schneiderman, was unable to tell me if the purchaser of the newspaper had a foreign accent or not.

"Also, as per your instructions, I visited the Baconburg Museum. In the stuffed-bird exhibit hall everything was normal and in place, except for the rare-birds-of-the-North-Atlantic exhibit. The stuffed giant puffin was missing. I questioned the guard about this—a Mr. Anolis—and it turned out that the bird had not yet been missed. It was evidently stolen. Mr. Anolis was of the opinion that it was a prank or practical joke, the bird being of no value except for purposes of study.

"I then consulted the Baconburg telephone directory, as you asked me to do, and discovered that there are exactly one hundred and fifty-two storage warehouses in the city. Of these, only twenty-five have areas in which the temperature can be thermostatically controlled; only eleven have proper cold-storage rooms; only three have twenty-four-hour access for customers; and only one, Roosman Brothers Storage Warehouse, has cold storage *and* round-the-clock access.

"I next contacted animal trainers around the city, and as

you predicted, there is an orangutan missing. It is a fifteen-year-old Sumatran male, the property of Shandar Eucalyptus, a circus performer. Mr. Eucalyptus was very upset about the missing orangutan and has offered a reward."

"Very interesting," said Osgood Sigerson. "And when did the animal disappear?"

"Yesterday," Ormond Sacker went on. "Mr. Eucalyptus informed me that the orangutan, named Howard, is a very obliging beast and will obey anyone.

"As to the other things you wanted me to check on: The coldest temperature in the nation yesterday was in Palmyra, New York, where it was an unseasonable twenty-six degrees Fahrenheit; no cargo planes have been chartered in the past three days; there are no rumors of major scandals in any European governments; the international currency market is normal; none of my underworld informants have seen a Panamanian dwarf with red hair; the films scheduled at the Snark Theater for tomorrow are both science-fiction ones, *Attack of the Pit People* and *Guacamole Monster* —they are both directed by the Mexican director Manuel Traneing—and your shirts will be back from the laundry on Thursday."

"Excellent, Sacker, excellent!" Osgood Sigerson said. "These are the pieces that complete the puzzle." All the time that Dr. Ormond Sacker had been talking, the world's greatest detective had been filling the room with clouds of dense, sickening pipe smoke. I wasn't sure, but I thought it might have been scented with avocado. To make matters worse, Rat had gotten out her cigarette holder and black cigarettes and was adding to the stink. I sat there helplessly. None of what Ormond Sacker was reporting made the least sense to me. I just took it all in and tried to keep from being sick; it was the avocado pie and Danish as much as the pipe smoke that was getting to me. I noticed that not only did Osgood Sigerson have a lot of pure white make-up on his face, not only were most of his hair and all of his sideburns painted on, but his nose was probably a fake.

"Young Miss Bentley Saunders Harrison Matthews, what do you know about the giant Indian fruit bat?" Osgood Sigerson asked, pointing his pipe at Rat.

"Well, they're the largest variety of bat," Rat said. "They eat fruit. They can have a wingspan of as much as six feet. And someone sends a stuffed one to my Uncle Flipping on his birthday every year."

"Aha!" Osgood Sigerson shouted. "It's one of the trademarks of that monster Nussbaum, as is the orangutan, by the way. That villain has left a trail of misery all over the world, marked by stuffed Indian fruit bats and stolen orangutans. We're up against the archfiend himself, Sacker, there's no doubt of it."

"Mr. Sigerson, what about my uncle?" Rat asked.

"Your uncle," Osgood Sigerson said sternly, "is in the greatest possible danger. There are no limits to what that devil Nussbaum will do. I could tell you a story about egg foo yung, but it's too horrible."

"My father told me that Nussbaum once kept a person in a vat of egg foo yung," Rat said.

"I was that person," Osgood Sigerson said. "After three days, I was able to make my escape. The egg foo yung is just one example of the cruelty of which Nussbaum is capable. We are up against no ordinary criminal. No decent person—not even I, who was his prisoner—has seen his face. He has a veritable empire of crime under his control. He can make things happen halfway around the world, just by whispering a single word. If I were capable of fear, I would be afraid of Nussbaum."

"Are we going to catch him?" Winston's uncle, the Mighty Gorilla asked. The Mighty Gorilla hadn't said very much all the time we had been in Osgood Sigerson's room, or hideout, or whatever it was. I hoped we'd get a chance to talk to him later. Maybe I would be able to get his autograph.

"Catch him?" Osgood Sigerson said. "I hope so. But the first thing to do is rescue Flipping Hades Terwilliger."

"Do you know where he is?" Dr. Ormond Sacker asked.

"I know exactly where he is," Osgood Sigerson said. "Mr. Gorilla, kindly bring the car around. There's no time to lose."

The Mighty Gorilla left. "Let's take some of these avocado eclairs with us," Osgood Sigerson said. "We may be on the hunt for a long time."

XXVI

Osgood Sigerson hurried us out a side door. We found ourselves outside Beanbender's Beer Garden. A shiny black car pulled up with the Mighty Gorilla at the wheel. Rat identified the car as a

1962 Studebaker Lark. The Mighty Gorilla was wearing a chauffeur's cap.

"Get in," said Osgood Sigerson. "We must make speed!"

We piled in. Rat and Dr. Ormond Sacker sat in the front with the Mighty Gorilla. Sigerson, Winston Bongo, and I sat in the back seat.

"Tell him where to go," Sigerson said to Dr. Sacker.

"Tell him?"

"Yes, tell him."

"I don't know where to tell him to go," Dr. Sacker said.

"Give Mr. Gorilla the address of Roosman Brothers Storage Warehouse," Sigerson snapped. "We're wasting valuable time here!"

Dr. Sacker gave the Mighty Gorilla an address. The Mighty Gorilla stepped on the gas. The powerful car surged forward. We blasted around a corner on two wheels, and the Mighty Gorilla pointed the glistening nose of the Lark toward the lights of Baconburg.

"Sacker, I should tell you that we may be going into some considerable danger," Osgood Sigerson said. "Have you got your lacrosse racquet with you?"

Dr. Ormond Sacker indicated a lacrosse racquet lying on the floor of the car and smiled a grim smile at Sigerson. To the rest of us, Sigerson said, "The doctor is the most dangerous man in America with a lacrosse stick."

"Mr. Sigerson," I asked, "will you tell us where we're going, and what you expect to find there?"

"I will explain as much as I can a bit later," Osgood Sigerson said. "For now, I suggest it would be best if we kept our minds clear for the dangerous action we will soon embark upon. If you like, I will enhance your education by giving a short talk on the history and manufacture of tennis balls."

Osgood Sigerson launched into a flood of facts about tennis balls. He evidently knew all there was to know about them and had a very good time relating all this knowledge to us.

Out of basic human decency, I will not relate what Sigerson said, or comment on it further, except to say that he kept it up all the way to Roosman Brothers Storage Warehouse.

The warehouse was located on a dark and deserted street on the south side of Baconburg. A single lightbulb burned over the door. The Mighty Gorilla brought the luxurious Studebaker to a stop directly in front of the door. There wasn't another car on the street. It was starting to rain.

We went inside. Near the door was a small desk where a night watchman or attendant should have been. There was no one in sight.

Then we heard a low moan. Sigerson spryly hopped over the desk and vanished behind it. In a moment we had all crowded around. Lying on the floor, bound hand and foot with what must have been a thousand feet of Scotch tape, was a man.

"Doctor, have a look at this poor fellow and tell us what you think," Sigerson said.

Doctor Sacker knelt over the figure. "He's not in too bad a condition," Sacker said. "He seems to have been struck with some force by a large, heavy object, something dense but not too hard, and with an irregular surface."

"Such as a pineapple?" Sigerson asked.

"Yes," Doctor Sacker said, "a pineapple would fit the

description. But why do you think this poor chap was hit with a pineapple?"

"Because here it is!" said Sigerson, holding up a somewhat bruised pineapple. "You will notice that there are various scraps of fruit here and there all over the office," Sigerson went on. "This was obviously the work of Howard, the orangutan kidnapped by Nussbaum. It will not have been the first innocent anthropoid set on a course of evil and criminality by Wallace Nussbaum. But you say that the watchman will recover?"

"Completely," said Doctor Sacker.

"Then let's go," Sigerson said. "I have no doubt that Nussbaum has long since fled, but we may find Flipping Hades Terwilliger, or some trace of him."

"Aren't we going to untie this poor fellow?" I asked.

"That's just what Nussbaum wants us to do," Sigerson said. "We'd be hours picking at the Scotch tape with our fingernails. No, we'll leave him as he is, resting comfortably. His coworkers will be along in a very few hours to help him."

Sigerson pushed a button and ushered us all into the service elevator. "Just taking a wild guess," he said, "I would say that the cold-storage rooms are on the top floor, close to the refrigeration equipment on the roof." He pushed the button for the top floor. Next to the button was a white card that said COLD-STORAGE ROOMS—TOP FLOOR.

"All of you wait here in the corridor," Sigerson said. "I'm going to reconnoiter."

Osgood Sigerson made his way down the corridor, sometimes crouching, sometimes almost crawling, sometimes flattening himself against the wall and listening intently. He disappeared around a corner. There wasn't a sound for a while. Then he was back.

"I've found it. You may all come with me," he said.

We followed the world's greatest detective down the hallway to an open door. "It's in here," Sigerson said. "There's no danger."

We entered a room that was intensely cold. It was a maze of electrical wires of every color, which hung in loops from the cooling pipes, snaked along the floor, and coiled up and down the walls. The wires were connected to various pieces of complicated-looking equipment, black boxes with switches and dials, digital readouts, TV screens, and blinking lights. In the middle of the room there was a large pile of straw surrounded by a crude wooden railing. On the pile of straw, about the size of the average kitchen stove, was something egg-shaped, dark green, and glistening. At various points, wires were plugged into the surface of the thing. A single shaded light fixture hung above the strange object, casting a strong illumination on it. The light fixture seemed to be swaying slightly, causing the shadow cast by the object to shift and move. It made the enormous avocadolike thing appear to be pulsating, breathing, alive.

"Gentlemen," Osgood Sigerson said, "the Alligatron! The only mature *Persea gigantica* in captivity!"

XXVII

"What *is* that thing?"
Rat asked.

"You mean it isn't obvious?" Osgood Sigerson replied. "This is a sort of quasi-kinetic-bionic-cybernetic device. In short, you might call it a vegputer."

"Oh," Rat said, "of course. Why didn't I know that right away? A vegputer! How simple! I have only one minor question: What on Earth is a vegputer, or, for that matter, a quasi-kinetic-bionic-cybernetic device?"

"Ah, I see how it is," said Osgood Sigerson. "Your scientific educations have been neglected. This has been one of the best-kept secrets of all time up until now, but I simply assumed that any high-school boy or girl would be able to figure out what this object is just by looking at the equipment surrounding it. I'll take a few moments to explain it to you."

Osgood Sigerson removed a number of pieces of wood from his pocket. Each one was a little bigger than a large lead pencil. The world's greatest detective screwed the bits of wood together end to end, making a long, thin stick, which he used as a pointer, indicating various parts of the Alligatron as he spoke.

"The Alligatron is, to put it as simply as possible, a gigantic avocado. All living things produce various exotic emanations—radio waves, electrical pulses, mysterious vibrations. In the case of members of the vegetable kingdom these emanations are quite weak and have generally been regarded as having no importance. The common or garden-variety alligator pear or avocado is well known to be the source of a surprising number of such emanations, for its size.

"Even so, the combined radiation, pulsation, and so forth of the average avocado do not amount to much and are barely measurable. In the case of this, the *Persea gigantica*, or giant avocado, the signals are much stronger. In fact, some years ago, working with an earlier hybrid much smaller than this one, the leading—and only—avocado researcher in the world, Mr. Flipping Hades Terwilliger, was able to cause a low-wattage lightbulb to flicker, powered by the electrical current present in the avocado.

"It was only when a very large avocado had been developed and more sophisticated monitoring techniques had been found that some really amazing discoveries were made.

"This enormous avocado is a living, thinking, feeling thing. By the way, it also makes a beautiful salad. The various items of equipment that I am now indicating with my pointer serve the purpose of monitoring and recording the, shall I say, thought processes of the vegetable part of the Alligatron. Other devices you see here are, in effect, amplifiers of certain electrical emanations of the avocado. Still others are controls, which stimulate certain functions of the giant fruit. And there are points of connection for still other devices that will help to project, or broadcast, the processes of this remarkable specimen.

"Obviously, strict temperature control is called for to keep the whole apparatus at peak operating efficiency—hence the refrigerated room. Once the avocado gets ripe and mushy, there's nothing to do but eat it. Yummy."

At this point, Osgood Sigerson stopped speaking and looked at the giant avocado as though he wanted to eat the whole thing then and there.

"Uh . . . Mr. Sigerson," I said.

"Yes, young Mr. Walter Galt," the world's greatest detective said.

"I just wanted to know . . . uh . . . why?"

"Why?"

"Yes, why make this complicated computer thing out of a giant avocado, assuming that it's even possible."

"Oh, it's more than possible," Osgood Sigerson said, dabbing his finger at the place where his false nose was coming loose. "It's a reality. As to why, I can give you a full explanation. An ordinary computer, while capable of elaborate operations, cannot produce actual thought waves. The Alligatron can not only produce thought waves of a very particular kind, but it can be made to project them.

"An Alligatron of this size has the thought power equal to that of seven hundred and fifty thousand licensed real-estate brokers—an apt comparison as there are now almost exactly seven hundred and fifty thousand licensed real-estate brokers in the continental United States."

"My mother thinks real-estate brokers are extraterrestrials," Rat said.

"She's perfectly correct," Osgood Sigerson said. "All licensed real-estate brokers are extraterrestrials—that is, they've all been taken over by extraterrestrial thought forms. And that, gentlemen and lady, is the purpose of the

Alligatron. Flipping Hades Terwilliger, working in secret, has evolved a way to repel these space invaders by counter-emanations of pure thought generated by the Alligatron. The natural frequency on which an avocado resonates is ideal for making contact with the thought forms that have taken control of our realtors."

"And Nussbaum?" Doctor Ormond Sacker asked.

"Obviously, Nussbaum is working on behalf of the invaders from space," Osgood Sigerson went on. "This place is Flipping Hades Terwilliger's secret laboratory. For some time, Mr. Terwilliger has been in the habit of suddenly disappearing for days at a time. It has been to this place that he has come on such occasions. He created an elaborate story of madness and pursuit by a master criminal to discourage inquiry. Of course, elements of his story were true—Wallace Nussbaum has been after him the whole time. However, through international contacts, such as Osgood Sigerson—that is, myself—Mr. Terwilliger was able to keep watch on Nussbaum's movements. While it isn't easy to catch Nussbaum, the police of four continents were able to keep sufficient pressure on the evil mastermind to prevent his coming to Baconburg for a time.

"Now, with Flipping Hades Terwilliger's research about to bear fruit, Nussbaum has made his move—a desperate break from cover—to try to wreck the Alligatron before it can be put to use to rid the world of the space realtors.

"Some months ago, Nussbaum dropped out of sight in the obscure Alpine village of Rackenbach. His trail remained cold until the American papers began to report a strange rash of orangutan thefts. Anyone versed in the history of crime could draw only one conclusion: Nussbaum was active in America.

"The trick was to find Mr. Terwilliger's secret laboratory before Nussbaum could. By the looks of it, we were only minutes too late. Still, there is hope. Nussbaum seems to have made off with Terwilliger, but has left the Alligatron intact. Possibly, he wants to keep it for himself in order to have power over the space realtors when the invasion is complete. This also argues well for the survival of Flipping Hades Terwilliger. Nussbaum will want to keep him alive and well to get the secret of the Alligatron from him."

"So the thing to do now . . ." said Doctor Ormond Sacker.

"The thing to do now is to find Nussbaum and get Flipping Hades Terwilliger back from him before any further damage is done," said Osgood Sigerson.

"Where do you think Nussbaum is?" Rat asked Osgood Sigerson, "and where do you think he has my uncle?"

"Yes," Doctor Ormond Sacker put in. "Hadn't we better go after them at once?"

"It's rather late," Osgood Sigerson said. "My suggestion is that we all repair to our various beds and have some rest. Tomorrow will be soon enough to go after that villain, Wallace Nussbaum."

"But you said that Nussbaum is dangerous," Winston Bongo said. "Shouldn't we try to get him before he does some harm to Flipping Hades Terwilliger?"

"It is just because Wallace Nussbaum is dangerous that we must take careful steps," Osgood Sigerson said. "Crime

fighters need their rest to do their best work. Although I
cannot but think that Mr. Terwilliger is having an unpleasant time of it, we must wait until tomorrow night. Then I
hope to have the pleasure of bringing Wallace Nussbaum,
that terrible malefactor, to justice at last."

It was arranged that the Mighty Gorilla would drive
Rat, Winston Bongo, and me home. Osgood Sigerson and
Dr. Ormond Sacker had a little bit of last-minute sleuthing
to do before they returned to their temporary secret head-
quarters. The following night, at eight, we were to meet
Osgood Sigerson in what he called "an amusing little restaurant." He pronounced the word *restaurant* with a sort
of French accent. The place was the Hasty Tasty, where
Winston and I had had a rubber doughnut at a time that
seemed long ago but had been, in reality, at the beginning
of this long night.

XXVIII

In the car going home we
finally got a chance to talk with the Mighty Gorilla. This
was what I had been waiting for all night. Of course, meeting the world's greatest detective and seeing the amazing
Alligatron had been very interesting, but the Mighty Gorilla was famous. He had wrestled all the strongest men in
the world. Besides, he was Winston's uncle.

"Yes, nephew," the Mighty Gorilla said, "I've worked for Mr. Sigerson a number of times—between athletic contests, of course. The first time I worked for him was in London. I was there, having just defeated the Horrible Fly. This Horrible Fly is a very popular European wrestler. He can walk up walls just like a fly, and his most effective hold consists of his actually dropping on you from the ceiling. He wears this helmet with big goggles over his eyes. It looks like he has flies' eyes. He's a very nice gentleman outside the ring. Well, I managed to pin the Horrible Fly, and then I met Mr. Sigerson. He needed a part-time bodyguard and driver while he worked on a case involving a giant Equadorian strangler.

"Another interesting wrestler I met was the Irish Bull. He was seven feet tall and weighed four hundred and sixty-seven pounds. I beat him, too, but it wasn't easy."

It was really interesting to listen to the Mighty Gorilla's stories. Before I got out of the car, I got him to autograph the greasy napkin from Beanbender's I had been carrying around in my pocket all night long.

It was just dawn when I got back to the apartment. My father was already awake, sitting in the breakfast nook, having a cup of tea. I had never known that he was such an early riser, although he was usually awake before I was.

"Hello, Walter," my father said. "Did you have fun looking for Flipping Hades Terwilliger?"

No one had actually said anything about keeping the events of the night secret from our own parents, but I had the general sense that I wasn't supposed to talk. I just said, "Yes, it was sort of interesting."

"Did you find him?" my father asked.

"Not yet," I said. "We're going to keep looking, starting again tonight."

"That's right," my father said. "You never find him in the daytime."

I felt like asking my father some questions about his own experiences in looking for Flipping Hades Terwilliger, but I suddenly realized that I was very tired. I was used to staying up most of the night, but sitting in the Snark Theater is very different from tramping all over town and racing around to secret laboratories with the world's greatest detective.

I wished my father a good night. He wished me a good morning, and I dragged myself off to bed.

XXIX

It was around two in the afternoon when my mother woke me up. "It's your no-good friend, Winston Bongo, on the telephone," she said. She always called him my no-good friend, except when she talked to him. Then she called me his no-good friend. "You might as well make plans for supper," my mother said. "Your father has to go to a meeting of the Association of Synthetic Sausage Manufacturers tonight, and I'm going to the Baconburg Ladies' Anti-Commonist Bridge League. If you and that other bum would like to fix yourselves something here, there's fresh tuna salad in the refrigerator."

I made my way to the telephone. "Hey, Winston," I said. "You want to eat out with me tonight? I thought we could go to Bignose's before we meet the others."

"Good idea," Winston said. "I think my mother is making krupnik or something again tonight." Winston's mother is a really awful cook. She's so bad that Winston tries to get invited to eat at my house whenever he can. To make matters worse, Mrs. Bongo is always taking cooking courses at the Baconburg Adult Education Center. Currently, she was taking a course in Polish cooking, but it wouldn't have mattered what nationality of cooking it was —she was sure to ruin whatever she made.

"Let's ask Rat if she wants to join us," I said.

"Fine. I'll call her and say it's your idea," Winston said. "I wouldn't want to give the impression that I'm asking for a date."

"I'll ring your bell at about six," I said.

"Okay," Winston Bongo said.

I hung up. My mother was polishing the plastic carpet runner. "I just want you to know that I don't approve of any of this all-night-long foolishness," she said. "For some unexplained reason, your father seems to think it's good for you to stay up to all sorts of hours, looking for that loony tune, Flipping Hades Terwilliger. He's always been crazy, you know. See that you don't get too near him."

My mother thinks craziness is catching, like a cold. Ordinarily, I might have given her an argument—and lost— but this time I was more interested in something else she'd said.

"Do you know Flipping Hades Terwilliger?" I asked.

"Sure, I know him," my mother said. "He's batty. He and your father were the only two members of the Avocado Club in high school—but it was all Flipping's idea. Your father is no bugbrain. He's completely sane, responsible, and *compos mentis*, take it from me. He could probably have been a senator or something if he didn't associate with muffinheads like Terwilliger. It looks as though you're going to turn out just the same, running around as you do with that Bolshevik, Winston Bongo."

"Winston's no Bolshevik," I said.

"Of course he's not going to admit it," my mother said, "but I'm keeping my eye on him just the same. If he ever gives you any literature, pamphlets or anything, you bring them straight to me, you hear?"

"Aw, Mom, Winston never gave me any pamphlets," I said.

"He's waiting for the opportune moment," my mother said. "There's no point in your trying to protect him. Just promise me that if he ever starts talking politics with you, you'll call the nearest FBI."

My mother went back to work on the plastic carpet runner, and I wandered back to my room to try to clear my head after the conversation with my mother. The phone rang again. I went to answer it. By this time, my mother was vacuuming the ceiling, and I could hardly hear whoever was on the other end.

It turned out to be Winston Bongo. He was calling to say that Rat wouldn't be joining us at Bignose's. It seemed that there was some kind of commotion or emergency at her house, and she would meet us at eight at the Hasty Tasty with the others. However, Winston said, he'd heard from his uncle, the Mighty Gorilla. The Mighty Gorilla had planned to eat at Winston's house before going to the Hasty Tasty, about which he apparently knew, but when he'd found out that his sister was going to try out a new recipe, he had lost his nerve and had decided to eat with us at Bignose's.

What was more, the Mighty Gorilla was going to pick us up in the powerful Studebaker Lark limousine, and we'd ride to Lower North Aufzoo Street in style.

The whole evening promised to be pretty exciting. I felt really grown-up and special. Here I was going to eat supper with an important celebrity and be driven there in a fancy car besides. Then I'd go to a meeting with the world's greatest detective and maybe get to help in the capture of a criminal mastermind.

I decided I'd better get spruced up. I went to take a shower, after which I was going to put on my special shirt that my father brought back from Hawaii when he was in the army.

We got the royal treatment at Bignose's. Bignose recognized the Mighty Gorilla at once and made a big fuss over him. The Mighty Gorilla had to promise Bignose six or seven times that he would be sure to mail him an autographed picture. Bignose said he would frame the picture and hang it up behind the cash register.

We didn't have to slide our trays along the shelf made of chrome tubing and pick out what we wanted to eat. That was too bad, because I actually like that part. Instead, Bignose put on a clean apron and waited on us at one of the tables. It certainly is different when you go places with somebody famous.

The food was incredible. It was more than incredible. It was beyond the power of words. It was . . . well, let me put it this way, it changed my life. Winston Bongo's, too. This is what Bignose served us: some kind of a salad made with dandelion greens, a sort of baked lamb with lots of herbs and garlic and a kind of cheese sprinkled on top, and roast potatoes. There was also a freshly baked whole-wheat bread with a crunchy crust and sesame seeds on it. For dessert there were Napoleons and cups of rich coffee with lots of cream.

It was good cooking. That's what changed my life, and Winston's. Both of us had been victims of bad cooking since we were babies. Gradually, we realized that the food at home was horrible. We got clues from things like being the only kids in school who liked the school-cafeteria food better than what we got at home. We both had experienced food outside our homes at various times, and it had always tasted better. Of course, our mothers were well-meaning —just very untalented—and what we got at home contained all the recommended vitamins, minerals, calories, and all that, and we were able to eat it, which not everyone could do. Our mothers certainly meant us no harm; they just couldn't cook. Now, of course both Winston and

I had found plenty to eat outside our homes, and there were all sorts of things we liked, but most of it was on the order of snacks and junk. What Winston and I experienced that night at Bignose's in the company of the famous Mighty Gorilla was *good cooking*, and it was the first time either of us had ever had it.

Needless to say, the wonderful food put us into a very good mood, and we had a superior time, sitting around and listening to the stories of the Mighty Gorilla, and feeling important and grown-up. Bignose asked if he could sit with us and listen to the Mighty Gorilla's stories for a while. Everybody else in the cafeteria wished they could be sitting with us, too. You could tell from the way they watched us the whole time we were there.

I neglected to mention that the Mighty Gorilla is a very stylish person. He had on a suit with red-and-black checks about two inches square. Also, he has flaming red hair that stands straight up, and an interesting red nose. He wears a monocle, and he carries a cane—it's actually more of a club. Of course, Winston's uncle has been to Europe and everyhere, so he knows how to dress.

With Bignose sitting with us, it was impossible to discuss the case we were working on with Osgood Sigerson, so we kept the conversation sort of general. Mostly we talked about wrestling. All of us had questions about wrestlers we had seen on television, and the Mighty Gorilla knew all of them. He also told us about wrestlers in Japan and Australia and other places he had been. As we sat there with the Mighty Gorilla and Bignose, neither Winston nor I could have decided which was more glorious—to be a wrestler or to be a cook.

By the time we set out in the luxurious Lark limousine for our meeting with Osgood Sigerson, Dr. Ormond Sacker, and Rat at the Hasty Tasty, we were all feeling pretty good. It was because of the wonderful meal at Bignose's.

"I hope this Nussbaum guy puts up a fight," Winston Bongo said. "I'd like to show Uncle Gorilla how strong I am."

"Personally, I hope there isn't any violence," the Mighty Gorilla said, "but if there's a need for any strong-arm stuff, I'll let you handle it, nephew."

"Good," Winston said. "I feel as though I could wrestle an elephant."

"If it should happen that you have to wrestle an orang-utan, which is more likely, be sure it doesn't get a hold on your feet," the Mighty Gorilla said. "Orangs are natural geniuses at wrestling, and if one gets hold of your feet, it's all over."

It was wonderful how much the Mighty Gorilla knew about wrestling. You could learn a lot just hanging around with him.

"The best orangutans for wrestling purposes come from the island of Maggasang in the Java Sea," the Mighty Gorilla said. "If one of those babies gets you by the foot, look out!"

The great car silently came to a stop outside the Hasty Tasty. We went inside. Osgood Sigerson was sitting alone at one of the tables.

"Good evening gentlemen," said the world's greatest detective. "You are just on time. I expect Miss Bentley Saunders Harrison Matthews, the female you affectionately call

Rat, to arrive at any moment. My colleague Dr. Sacker may be a bit late. Meanwhile, I invite you to enjoy the offerings of this excellent establishment. The specialty of the house is raisin toast. Karl, the chef, is famous for it. I am just starting on my third helping. I recommend it."

I had my misgivings about eating anything in the Hasty Tasty, remembering the rubber doughnut. To be polite, I ordered some raisin toast and a cup of coffee. Winston and the Mighty Gorilla did the same.

To nobody's surprise, the raisin toast was horrible and the coffee was undrinkable.

"Aren't you going to eat that?" Osgood Sigerson asked, snatching the intact-except-for-one-bite stack of raisin toast from my plate. "There's no sense letting it go to waste. I'll eat it."

As a general rule, I don't eat raisin toast. I don't know anybody who does, except my father. Maybe it's a taste that goes with liking avocados.

Rat showed up. She looked excited, as though she had something remarkable to tell us. Before she could speak, Osgood Sigerson held up a finger for silence.

"Good evening, young Miss Matthews," he said. "Correct me if I am wrong, but were you not about to tell us that Heinz, the Chinese butler at your family's home, has disappeared without a trace?"

"Yes!" said Rat, amazed. "But how did you know that?"

"Tut! It is elementary," said Osgood Sigerson, "but I will not take time to tell you how I know about his disappearance just now. Instead, I will tell you something equally surprising. My esteemed friend and companion, Dr.

Ormond Sacker, has also vanished. He's gone without a trace, a thing he has never been known to do before."

"That's terrible," I said.

"It is also significant," said the world's greatest detective. "A well-trusted family retainer vanishes, and my well-trusted friend and companion vanishes. There's bound to be a connection between these two strange events, but we'll get back to that later. At the moment, I want to tell you all how I spent my day."

XXXI

Osgood Sigerson got out one of his horrible pipes and began to speak. "As all of you know, the main commerical street of the Old Town is Nork Avenue. This street intersects Budhi Street at the very center of the bohemian and artistic district. Here, all sorts of unconventional persons congregate. There are painters and writers, scholars and actors, as well as many others who exist on the fringe of well-regulated society.

"The absolute center—the navel, so to speak—of this busy community is the Nor-Bu Drug Company, located on the northeast corner of the intersection I have mentioned. It is to the Nor-Bu Drug Company that the residents of the artists' quarter repair, not only to have their prescriptions filled, acquire baby oil, cigars, note paper, magazines, ear plugs, boxes of cheap candy for their loved ones, water wings, household solvents, paperback books, toothbrushes, postcards, and souvenirs of Baconburg, but to partake of the food and drink, and society, at the famous Nor-Bu Drug Company soda fountain. It is here, at the long marble counter, that the artistic and intellectual lights of the city sit all day, drinking cola and reading the New York papers. It is the best place in Baconburg to engage in conversation—and to gather information.

"I should say that in addition to the various practitioners of the arts who frequent the soda fountain at the Nor-Bu Drug Company, many stool pigeons, card sharpers, bunco steerers, dacoits, cutpurses, granny bashers, yobs, and unlicensed librarians also congregate there. These representatives of the criminal class favor the strawberry malteds for which the Nor-Bu is justly famous.

"So it was that I, disguised as a gentleman thug, spent the day in pleasant conversation with the artistic and criminal fringe of society. My object, of course, was to find out what I could about our friend Mr. Nussbaum. In the course of chatting with my fellow devotees of the strawberry malted, I also got wind of a major bank robbery that is being planned, and I was invited to join a ring of bus thieves. All this will be reported to the authorities when I have a free moment."

"But what about Nussbaum?" the Mighty Gorilla broke in. "Did you find anything out about him?"

"And what about my uncle, Flipping Hades?" Rat asked.

"And what about Dr. Sacker?" I asked.

"In a word," Osgood Sigerson continued, "my interviews with the colorful clients of the Nor-Bu Drug Company were rewarding. By the way, did you know that there's a talented painter in this city who has done a picture of his bedroom with every object that is moveable removed and every stationary object painted white? It's quite a concept. And people say there's no good art in the provinces! Now, where was I? Oh, yes! Nussbaum has Flipping Hades as his captive. That's certain. And I very nearly know where. As to Dr. Sacker, I can't think what's become of him. He was in and out of the Nor-Bu all day, disguised as a disqualified Mexican bullfighter. The last I saw of him, he was in the act of shadowing a suspicious man in a beret. Sacker thought he had the build of an orangutan. I didn't agree. The fellow came in to buy cough drops and had the look of a Ceylonese orchestra leader. I'm seldom wrong in judging a person's occupation and place of origin, but Sacker insisted and followed the fellow when he left."

"Did you happen to notice what flavor of cough drops the man in the beret bought?" the Mighty Gorilla asked.

"Certainly. Tangerine Eucalyptus," Osgood Sigerson said.

"It could have been an orangutan," the Mighty Gorilla said, "that's the flavor they like. They're the devil if they get you by the feet."

"Of course, I could have been mistaken," Osgood Sigerson said. "There's a first time for everything. Still, I hardly think I'd be likely to make such an elementary mistake."

At that moment, Dr. Sacker rushed in. He was out of

breath and appeared to be very excited. "Sigerson!" he gasped, dropping heavily into a chair, "it *was* an orangutan! I have definite proof!"

"Possibly," Osgood Sigerson said, "but what proof could you have? Remember, there are many people who have a funny way of walking."

"Here's the proof!" Dr. Ormond Sacker said, and triumphantly handed Osgood Sigerson a newspaper clipping.

I read the clipping over Osgood Sigerson's shoulder. It had a picture of an orangutan and was all about the disappearance of Adolph, an orangutan who had previously lived in the zoo in Colombo, Sri Lanka, the country that used to be called Ceylon. The article said that Adolph was a genius among orangutans, and that he had great musical talent. In fact, on a number of occasions, the ape had conducted the Sri Lanka National Orchestra. He specialized in the work of German Romantic composers.

"This clipping proves that *I* was right!" Osgood Sigerson said.

"What do you mean?" Dr. Ormond Sacker asked. "I said that it was an orangutan, and you said it wasn't."

"I said it was a Ceylonese orchestra conductor," Osgood Sigerson said, "and if this clipping is correct, so was I. I do admit that you were partly right in that you noticed that the suspect in question was an orangutan, but that is a minor point. The outstanding thing about him is that he *was* the conductor of a Ceylonese orchestra."

"The outstanding thing about him is that he led me to the place where Nussbaum is hiding!" Dr. Ormond Sacker shouted triumphantly.

"He did?" Rat, Winston Bongo, the Mighty Gorilla, and I all asked excitedly.

"Of course he did," Osgood Sigerson said coolly. "You must forgive me, Sacker, my dear fellow, but I have this irresistible urge for dramatics and indirection. I'm afraid I played on your little weaknesses of personality once again. Of course, I saw that it was an orangutan right away. Anybody could have seen that. The reason I argued with you was in order to prompt you to follow the creature, thinking it was your own idea. I mean no offense, old man, but you have a perfectly terrible shadowing technique—except when you are angry and trying to prove a point. Then you're just like a bloodhound. I insisted that the creature wasn't an orangutan just to make you mad enough to stick to his heels like grim death."

"You mean you knew it was really an orangutan all the time?" Dr. Ormond Sacker asked, crestfallen.

"The Sri Lankan government consulted me about that case weeks ago," Osgood Sigerson said. "Now cheer up, old fellow, nobody could have followed him as well as you did."

"Oh, really, Sigerson," Dr. Ormond Sacker said, blushing, "you're too kind. Anybody could have done it."

"You're lucky he didn't grab you by the foot," the Mighty Gorilla said. "There's no getting out of it when one of those orangs gets you by the foot."

XXXII

"Dr. Sacker, you said that the orangutan led you to the place where Wallace Nussbaum is hiding," Winston Bongo said.

"Yes, that's right," Dr. Ormond Sacker said. "At least, I am fairly sure he did. I didn't see Nussbaum—not that I know what he looks like—but it stands to reason. This was the progression of my logical deductive thought: One, here is an orangutan that disappeared some time ago under mysterious circumstances—an orangutan, I might add, with no reason to leave his previous situation, a celebrity, a famous orchestra conductor. Two, who is it that has a strange, mysterious, mystical power over orangutans? Wallace Nussbaum! Three, Nussbuam is known by my distinguished colleague Sigerson to be in this city—only recently an orangutan has been abducted right here in Baconburg. Four, now an orangutan that disappeared in a city in Asia appears here in Baconburg. I submit that the beast is working for Nussbaum, and that it will lead us to him, if it has not already done so. It stands to reason, does it not?"

"Good work, Sacker," Osgood Sigerson said. "I'll make a detective of you yet. You worked that out almost exactly as I had already done."

"You mean you had already figured all this out?" Dr. Ormond Sacker asked the world's greatest detective.

"Elementary," said Osgood Sigerson. "Would I be the world's greatest detective if I hadn't?"

"Sigerson, you're a genius!" Dr. Ormond Sacker said.

"That is true," Osgood Sigerson said.

"Mr. Sigerson, do you think that the disappearance of our butler, Heinz, is connected with all of this?" Rat asked.

"I am certain of it," said Osgood Sigerson, "and now let us waste no more time in idle theorizing. I give to my dear friend Dr. Sacker the honor of telling you where the orangutan led him, a fact already known to me."

"Sigerson, there's no one like you!" Doctor Ormond Sacker exclaimed warmly, "and thank you for the honor of being the one to tell. The orangutan led me to the Sausage Center Building."

"That's where my father works!" I shouted. The Sausage Center Building is the largest building in Baconburg. It looks like a giant castle or fort. In it are the offices of a whole lot of sausage manufacturers, the National Sausage Council, the editorial offices of *Sausage* magazine, and downstairs on the ground level is The Smiling Sausage, which is a restaurant. Nobody actually makes sausages in the Sausage Center Building, but every office in the building has something to do with sausages. My father has his own company, Galt's Synthetic Sausages. He is one of the few sausage manufacturers whose product contains no meat at all. In fact, they are made entirely in the laboratory. My father sells them mostly to restaurants, especially those places along the toll roads.

"The Sausage Center Building is exactly right!" Osgood Sigerson said. "Now, would you like to tell our friends exactly where in the Sausage Center Building the orangutan led you?"

"Certainly, old friend," Doctor Ormond Sacker said. "In the Sausage Center Building there is a movie theater, which is no longer in use. I saw the orangutan enter the theater through a side door. I followed him no farther, but hurried back here to make my report, although, of course, you already knew all of this, Sigerson."

"Enough talk!" Osgood Sigerson said. "The time has come for action! Into the car, everybody! The game's afoot!"

"Those orangutans get a hold on our feet, we'll all be in trouble," the Mighty Gorilla said.

The powerful car sped along silently. We all sat in grim silence. Finally, Osgood Sigerson spoke. "This is it. I can feel it. The archfiend Wallace Nussbaum is almost in my grasp."

The Sausage Center Building loomed in the darkness before us. I could hardly hear anyone breathing. My mouth felt dry. The Mighty Gorilla cracked his knuckles. Osgood Sigerson adjusted his false nose. I remember wondering at that tense moment how he came to lose his actual nose. It must have been in a desperate struggle with some fiendish criminal, unless, of course, the false nose was merely a disguise to confuse his enemies.

"We'll go through a window," Osgood Sigerson said. "Sacker, do you know where the disused movie theater is located?"

"I think it is over at that end of the building, on the

ground floor," Dr. Ormond Sacker said, indicating the place with his lacrosse racquet.

"Bring the car to a stop over there, Mr. Gorilla," Osgood Sigerson said, "and I warn you all, not a sound!"

We followed Osgood Sigerson in single file without making a noise. The world's greatest detective sprang like a cat to a window ledge, took something out of his pocket, and with a tiny clicking noise picked the lock and slid the window open. He then motioned for us to stay below in the street and vanished inside.

In a few minutes, he reappeared and motioned for us to follow. One by one we scrambled up to the ledge, and Osgood Sigerson helped each of us inside. Soon we had all assembled in a small, dark room.

"This is perfect," Osgood Sigerson whispered. "We are in a storeroom at the back of the theater. Through that door is the projection booth, and through that one, the auditorium. There is a short flight of steps going up to the projection room and a step or two down into the auditorium. From this vantage point, we will be able to observe, or at least hear, all that goes on. At present, the theater seems to be empty. Now, I suggest that we all take positions behind these boxes and packing crates and wait in utter silence. I caution all of you not to make a move without my signal. And not a sound! This may be the greatest danger any of us has experienced. Now, quickly, all find hiding places!"

I squeezed into a space between a sort of locker or broom closet and a corner. Rat and Winston crouched behind a large box. The Mighty Gorilla knelt down behind a thing like a canvas laundry hamper on wheels. Dr. Ormond Sacker disappeared behind a file cabinet, and Osgood Sigerson silently slid a bookcase a few inches away from the wall and slipped behind it.

A very dim glow from a distant streetlamp kept the room from being totally dark. Still, even after I'd had plenty of time to get used to the darkness, all I could make out were indistinct dark shapes.

We waited in silence for what seemed forever. My knee was getting stiff, and I itched in places I couldn't reach. Even though the room was cold, sweat trickled down my back. I tried to practice silent breathing. Apparently everybody else was doing that, too, because there wasn't a sound in the room.

I could hear the ticking of my watch. It sounded as loud as a drum. I slipped it off and put it in my pocket. My nose itched; I prayed that I wouldn't sneeze. An hour must have gone by, maybe two. My feet were numb.

Then I suddenly felt ice cold all over. Something was moving outside the room. Something was making a noise. It was a rasping, shuffling, sliding sound. It was getting closer. Whatever was making that noise, I knew I didn't want to see it.

Then I saw it. The door to the auditorium opened and, framed in the dim light from the empty theater, I saw a hideous shape. It was the size of a big man, as big as the Mighty Gorilla, but shorter, with short, bowed legs. The head of the thing was large and ragged looking and topped by a sort of smooth, rounded shape. I smelled a faint, sweetish odor. Bananas. I realized that I was looking at an orangutan wearing a raincoat and a beret. The creature was much larger than I had imagined. It hesitated, closed the door behind itself, and shuffled to the other door, the one leading to the projection room. It went through the door and shut it.

I was pretty shaken up after my first look at the orangutan. I never got a chance to get hold of myself, because the next thing to happen was a really bloodcurdling fiendish laugh that came from the auditorium.

"So, my dear Mr. Flipping Hades Terwilliger, you still don't want to talk, is that so?" said someone in the auditorium. The voice was evil-sounding, cruel, and also somehow familiar. I couldn't place it. "You won't talk?" the voice continued. "How would you like to see *Das Dreimaederlhaus* for the sixth time?"

"The monster!" I heard Osgood Sigerson whisper. "He's forcing him to watch German movies!"

"Shall I have Adolph roll the film?" the fiendish voice asked, "or are you ready to talk? After this comes seventy-two hours of German comedies."

"This is too inhuman," Sigerson said under his breath. "We have to rush those vile torturers before that poor man has to watch another foot of film. Sacker! You and the young people will burst into the auditorium and neutralize Nussbaum with the lacrosse racquet. Mr. Gorilla and I will go into the projection booth and deal with Adolph."

"Let's see," the evil-sounding voice went on. "This one is called *Funny Jokes in Dusseldorf*. Here's another called *Laughs and Stunts on the Riviera*, and this one sounds good, *Hilarious Clowns on the Farm*. You'll have to watch all of these, Mr. Flipping Hades Terwilliger. Don't you want to talk and spare yourself a lot of horrible pain?"

"You don't realize who you're dealing with, you criminal," we heard Flipping Hades Terwilliger say. "I'll never reveal the secret of the Alligatron!"

"Adolph!" Nussbaum shouted. "Roll the film!"

"Rush the doors!" Osgood Sigerson whispered. "*Now!*"

XXXIII

It all happened so fast. There was no time to think. I've heard people say about battles in war and accidents and things like that that there was no time to be scared. I was scared plenty, but I moved forward with the others on Osgood Sigerson's signal.

Sigerson and the Mighty Gorilla bounded through the door into the projection room, where Adolph, the orangutan orchestra conductor from Ceylon who had been abducted by Wallace Nussbaum and turned to crime, stood. Dr. Ormond Sacker, brandishing his lacrosse racquet, burst through the door into the auditorium with Rat, Winston Bongo, and myself crowding after him.

It turned out to be perfect timing. At the very moment we entered the theater, the lights went out and the screen became illuminated with the first frames of the German movie with which Wallace Nussbaum intended to torture Flipping Hades Terwilliger.

Coming into the movie house through a door in the corner at the end farthest from the screen, we got a perfect view of everything. There was someone sitting in the very first row, right in the middle. That would be Flipping Hades. Standing to one side, his back to the screen and his face horribly distorted by the light from the projector, was Nussbaum. I didn't have time to study him. Dr. Sacker didn't hesitate for a moment. He thundered down the aisle, waving the lacrosse stick and bellowing, "Spread out! Cover the exits! Don't let him get away! Shoot to kill!"

Nobody had anything to shoot with, as far as I knew, but we did spread out, Winston sprinting across the theater through a row of seats. Rat followed him about halfway, and I ran along behind Dr. Sacker.

"Surrender, you scoundrel!" Dr. Sacker shouted. "Get the tear gas and the nets ready, men! Don't release the dogs until I give the order! Arf! Arf! Woof! Grrrr!"

Then Dr. Sacker began blowing on a police whistle. There was a lot of shouting going on. Everybody was shouting and screaming. I was doing it, too, I discovered.

"Don't eat meat! Don't eat meat!" I screamed at the top of my lungs.

All this happened in a few seconds. Nussbaum, blinded by the light of the projector and confused by all the shouting and whistling, hesitated for a moment. His face was alternately brown, green, red, and blue as it picked up colors from the German movie, the soundtrack of which was blaring, adding to the confusion.

There were shouts and noises coming from above, too. In the projection room, a horrible battle was taking place. I felt my heart sink when I heard the Mighty Gorilla's voice cry out, "Oh, Lordy, he's got me by the foot."

We were almost upon him when Nussbaum got his bearings. He put his head down and ran like a football player, first to the right, toward Dr. Sacker and me, then, suddenly changing direction, he vaulted over a row or two of seats, shifted to the left, and began to sprint up the other aisle toward Winston Bongo.

Dr. Sacker, Rat, and I began to cross the theater, going as fast as we could sideways, down three separate rows of seats. Before any of us could get across, Nussbaum, now visible only as a fiendish silhouette, encountered Winston Bongo.

Winston was in a wrestling stance, arms and legs spread wide apart, head lowered, knees bent, blocking Nussbaum's progress up the aisle. Nussbaum hesitated, and then reached inside his coat. He pulled out an object—I couldn't tell exactly what it was, but I later learned that it was a stuffed Indian fruit bat—which he raised above his head, making ready to bash Winston.

"Oh no! He's going to brain him!" I shouted.

Winston made a deft, understated movement, a sort of half turn, crouch, and feint with his right hand.

Nussbaum left the floor and described a half circle in the air, landing on his back. In the next instant we were all upon him. Dr. Sacker sat heavily on Nussbaum's chest, holding the lacrosse stick across his neck and growling, "Arf! Arf! Woof!" Winston dropped to his knees and busied himself tying Nussbaum's feet together with his belt. Rat and I each grabbed one of the master criminal's hands.

The house lights went on, and Osgood Sigerson appeared, sauntering down the aisle as though he were out for a morning stroll. Following him was the Mighty Gorilla, whose red-and-black-checked suit was badly rumpled and torn in places.

"That went very well, did it not?" the world's greatest detective said. He picked up Nussbaum's discarded Indian fruit bat. "I will keep the miscreant covered with this," Sigerson said, "while one of you boys unties Mr. Terwilliger. He must be very uncomfortable, trussed up like that."

XXXIV

"Mildred," my father shouted, "I can't find my gold-plated collar button anywhere." He was on his hands and knees, looking under furniture in the bedroom. My father is possibly the last man on earth who uses collar buttons. He has these shirts made without collars. At the front and the back there are these little buttonholes. The collar is separate, and you button it on. I think this kind of shirt started to go out of style about a hundred years ago. My father gets them somewhere, and he keeps his collar buttons, which look sort of like tacks with a little ball where the point should be, in an old nose-putty can.

I could hear him hollering for help while searching for the gold-plated collar button as I sat in my room, labeling a picture of an earthworm for the biology notebook.

Everything was back to normal.

That night, I planned to Snark Out with Winston and Rat. We still Snarked pretty often, but we no longer kept score. Tonight's films were *The Hound of the Baskervilles* and *Sherlock Holmes Faces Death*, two first-raters.

It was hard to believe that not very long before I had been present on that night of excitement, terror, and violence when we captured Wallace Nussbaum, the international archfiend and king of crime.

The most exciting thing to happen since that night was that my father, without my knowledge, had slipped a slice of avocado into a bologna sandwich he made me, and I had eaten it, and I liked it. This made him very happy. Still, I am not a fanatic like him. For example, I am not going with him to the annual American Avocado Fancier's convention, unless it's definite that Osgood Sigerson is going to be there. My father thinks that Sigerson won't come. Apparently, they've never met. Sigerson seems to make it to the convention only every other year, and somehow those years my father doesn't go. He goes to the Sausage Maker's Association convention instead, which takes place the same week.

My mind went back to that night in the deserted movie theater in the Sausage Center Building. I could see it all as clearly as if it were happening right before my eyes.

"Let's unmask him," Osgood Sigerson had said.

"Unmask him? What do you mean?"

"Nussbaum! He's evidently disguised," said the world's greatest detective. "Doctor, just give that beard a tug and peel off those eyebrows, and we'll see what we have."

Dr. Ormond Sacker pulled gingerly at Nussbaum's beard. It came right off. So did the eyebrows, revealing—

"Heinz!" Rat shouted.

"Swine!" Wallace Nussbaum hissed at Osgood Sigerson. "You haven't done with me yet!"

"That remains to be seen," said Osgood Sigerson. "At the present moment, trussed up as you are with my good friend Sacker's extra-strong shoelaces, I'd say that I've very nearly done with you—at least I will have when the police arrive to arrest you."

"Arrest me? On what charge?" the archfiend asked, sneering.

"Orangutan rustling will do for the moment," Osgood Sigerson said. "The poor beast tied up with electric cord in the projection room should be evidence enough to have you sent away for a number of years. People in this part of the world don't look kindly on orangutan rustling, Nussbaum."

"I thought I was finished when that brute got me by the foot," the Mighty Gorilla said. "How did you ever subdue him, Mr. Sigerson?"

"Some years ago," the detective said, "I took some lessons in baritsu, or the Japanese system of wrestling. As I recall, I answered an advertisement on the back of a magazine. That instruction stood me in good stead this night. I will write a letter to the baritsu master of Piscataway, New Jersey, offering my thanks and endorsing his method. That should result in his becoming a very rich man."

All this time, Rat and Flipping Hades Terwilliger were standing amazed, speechless. Finally, Rat spoke. "Heinz! Heinz is Nussbaum? I can't believe it!"

"Yes, it was the butler," Osgood Sigerson said. "I knew it all along."

"Nussbaum, you monster," Dr. Ormond Sacker said. "You'll do no more damage now."

"We'll see about that," said the master criminal.

"And how are you feeling?" Osgood Sigerson asked Flipping Hades Terwilliger.

"I never felt better in my life," said Rat's uncle. "I could have held out for weeks. What this poor fool didn't know is that I *like* German movies. I had already seen *Das Drei-maederlhaus* ten or fifteen times voluntarily. It's almost my favorite movie, after *Maedchen in Uniform*."

Sigerson shuddered involuntarily. "You're a man of peculiar tastes, Terwilliger," he said.

"My only worry," Flipping Hades Terwilliger said, "was that Nussbaum, frustrated because I would not reveal to him the secret of operating the Alligatron, might destroy it. Tell me, is my masterpiece all right? It would take ten years at least to grow another avocado of sufficient power."

"The Alligatron is perfectly safe," Osgood Sigerson said. "We saw it only last night, and it appears to be intact."

At this point, Wallace Nussbaum collapsed in a fit of hysterical laughter. "Fools! Fools! You are undone!" he shrieked. "Oh, this gives me so much pleasure! You have forgotten Howard, my other orangutan, my newest helper! Howard has been given instructions to utterly destroy your accursed machine, Terwilliger! By this time he is certain to have completely wrecked the thing and has probably eaten half of it." Nussbaum's face was contorted in an expression of evil glee. "Go! Have him arrested. He won't put up much of a fight, stuffed to the gills with avocado as he is. So, you see, I have the last laugh! Terwilliger, your Alligatron is no more!"

"Sigerson! Can this be true?" Dr. Ormond Sacker asked.

"Of course it can!" Osgood Sigerson snapped. "Why didn't you remind me about Howard? Do I have to think of everything myself? This was almost a perfect case, except for your bungling, you nitwit!"

"Sigerson, please forgive me," Dr. Sacker said.

"Of course, old fellow," the world's greatest detective said. "I keep forgetting that no one is as intelligent as I am. The fault is mine."

"Oh, Sigerson, you're too good," Ormond Sacker said.

"Yes, I am," said Sigerson.

"But," I said, "if the Alligatron is destroyed, that means there is no way to repel the extraterrestrial thought forms that have invaded Earth by taking over the bodies of every licensed realtor in the United States."

"I'm afraid that's right," Flipping Hades Terwilliger said.

"But that means every licensed realtor in America is a creature from outer space!" I shouted. "What are we going to do about it?"

"Well," said Osgood Sigerson, the world's greatest detective, "I suppose we'll just have to live with it."

DANIEL PINKWATER is a serious author of books for young people, which is to say, he doesn't do anything else worth mentioning, unless you count drawing pictures for said books.

The publication of this book celebrates the awarding to Daniel Pinkwater of the coveted Leonard Prize for Literature.

The Leonard Prize for Literature is bestowed by Steve Leonard, who attends school in Auburn, Washington. When asked why he had chosen to give this prestigious award to Mr. Pinkwater, Steve Leonard replied that it was "for all of his books, in particular *Lizard Music* and *Alan Mendelsohn, The Boy from Mars.*"